T0370415

Odalie Markette

Dr. Allen R. Remaley

authorHOUSE®

AuthorHouse™
1663 Liberty Drive
Bloomington, IN 47403
www.authorhouse.com
Phone: 833-262-8899

Published by AuthorHouse 09/10/2024

ISBN: 979-8-8230-3330-5 (sc)
ISBN: 979-8-8230-3329-9 (e)

Library of Congress Control Number: 2024918994

Print information available on the last page.

Other Books by Allen R. Remaley

The Hunter Model and Its Application
to Teaching Foreign Languages
A Hint of Jasmine and Lavender: An Erotic Romance
Susquehanna Odyssey
The Teacher's Playbook: A Guide to
Success in the Classroom
In the Shadow of Allah
The Awakening of Annie Hill
Letters Late: Things Left Unsaid
Midnight Lullaby: A Tender Tribute to a Woman
Muhammadville
Reflections of a Disgruntled American Gargoyle
The Magician
Ya Should'a Been There
The Tree Climber
"19"
The Dream Catcher
The Marilyn Chronicles: One Man's Effort to Become a
More-Understanding Dementia Care Giver for His Wife

Prologue

When Robert W. Service wrote his "The Cremation of Sam McGee", no one questioned how a man in the middle of a burning furnace could feel at home. That there are strange things done and witnessed in this world should not be a surprise; we know all too little about the place we call home, and we sheepishly exclaim surprise when some new discovery reveals things not before imagined or witnessed. This is a story of some people who embrace a special moment in time and place...and they kept that moment to themselves until now.

Odalie Markette

1

———⦉⦊———

Growing up in the little town of Blois, the historic habitat of French kings and queens, Odalie Markette was anything but nondescript. She had a maturity uncommon for one of her age. Before she was sixteen, she had completed her bac, that severe test which determines whether you will be a shop girl or a college graduate. Odalie would be a stellar student at Universite Grenoble, and her beauty was beyond comparison with others her age. That she was sought after by most of the young men on campus was common knowledge, but few would ever be able to say, "We became lovers."

But Odalie had one fascinating ability. She could scan a face, determine whether the person had ability, and with a little application of mentalism and an encouraging touch, she seemed to possess the magic of convincing a subject that his talent could be enhanced and lead to instant success. That ability even surprised Odalie in college. She had made the acquaintance of one of the university's soccer players, and within a few months, Grenoble University had won a sectional championship, and its prime player, Luc Plessy, had received offers to play for the Bleu, one of the prime teams in France. But there was a catch.

Odalie was adamant in her adherence to certain rules. If she were to use her uncanny ability to bring out a person's gift, no physical or romantic connections between subject and spell castor could take place. After a year of international soccer, Luc had become semi-rich. His first-year bonus of a million euros was shared with his muse, Odalie. But Luc Plessy made a fatal mistake. He seduced his teacher, the girl who had brought out a professional effort on his behalf. They had sex, and the following week, Plessy made the worst showing of his soccer career in a trial run in Paris. After a short deliberation of coaches and owners, Luc Plessy's career as a superstar soccer player as over, and he was sent home immediately.

Odalie Markette was not imprudent about love making. She was not shortsighted about such feelings, but she did know that, should anything involving touch and romance and its consequences produce a reversal of ability in her human specimen, she was and could not linger on such a thing. She then moved on to a different arena, and did not look back. Failed experiments began lining an abandoned road like broken-down and worn-out vehicles.

Odalie approached her subjects not as guinea pigs. Once chosen, once expectations had been outlined, agreed upon and put into motion, Odalie's chosen one became almost her child, and she became a mother who guided her new companion through the first steps to stardom. But she never lost sight of the fact that any close attachment to her made by her coached individual would be almost indecent and border on incest. Passion, however, is sometimes uncontrollable, and Odalie was a beautiful, voluptuous young woman, and she, too, had needs.

2

At the end of each adventure---the installation of some super belief that if followed, Odalie's advice and direction would lead to superstar status, Odalie would return to her home in Blois where she had purchased a little cottage at the edge of the Loire River. It was there that she had her base of operations much like Joan of Arc did in 1429. Joan had set up her own war room in Blois in defense of Orleans against the English. She, like Odalie, seemed to inspire men to do the impossible, and they did; they drove the English north and out of the Loire Valley. Odalie did not think of herself the equal to the female warrior of the fifteenth century. She could not explain what seemed to have been inspired by some supernatural source---the ability to help individuals reach and go beyond their potential. But her ability, whatever it was, was lucrative.

Odalie had built up a war chest of some wealth. Her soccer star, Luc, had given Odalie enough euros to buy her home and then some. In Blois, she had connections via newspapers and television to follow amateur sports, musical careers and stage and screen divas, and she was always on the verge of contacting those whose careers seemed to have hit a snag. It was usually at that point that Odalie Markette would appear, propose the unbelievable and convince her next protégé that something bordering the uncommon could make a difference in their life and future. Before too long, an opportunity was soon to come to light, and Odalie would once again use her magic on some up-and-coming superstar.

3

At the university, Odalie had dabbled in psychology and the science of the mind. She had studied the mental processes and what makes people tick. She knew a lot about the power of suggestion and how it worked, and she had perfected the idea of making someone believe that they could, with encouragement, plant a mental image of one's expectations in the mind. The subject, after time, would fall in love with the image projected and subconsciously be so fixed on the thing desired, that a polish, a luster and a competence would fall into place. But under no circumstances would the thing desired and its enabler be part of a romantic linking.

Odalie had practiced her scientific theories on children at a local day-care center. Children who had come to her with certain passions (learning to play the piano, being able to manipulate a soccer ball, sing in a more-mature voice, and solve advanced math problems), seemed to excel with Odalie's coaching. Supervisors at the day-care center pleaded with Odalie to pursue teaching as a career. She did just that, but her teaching would involve adult subjects who aspired to achieve more than ever thought possible. And, once the realization that profit could come from her endeavors, Odalie was off and running.

One of the first teaching methods Odalie used in her lessons to others was the concept of practice. Most people had heard and believed that the old adage of 'practice makes perfect' was the sure path to success in any field. Odalie knew that this was not true, and she understood that if a trade, profession or calling involved practicing something in the wrong way, that defect could only be corrected over long periods of time with the teacher showing that practice is only effective if perfect practice is outlined, i.e., there are correct ways to improve a skill, and that is by doing what is required in a perfect way.

Odalie had watched brick layers in and around Blois going about their job in a meticulous fashion. Bricks are laid not one atop the other, they are placed so that the top of one is placed on the seam of another. If not, the entire wall will topple in the slightest breeze. Practice can lead to perfection only if the proper procedures are followed. Odalie was astute enough to study what made practice perfect in various fields, and she applied that science to those who came to her for advice. In music, Odalie was musically dumb and deaf, but she knew the ins and outs of perfecting one's skills by reading, watching and cataloging what other successful people had done in their careers. The only magic Odalie possessed was that which she had studied. There was no black magic here. It was very thorough application of the scientific steps to success. But if applied with care, the results of Odalie's training and knowledge made people believe in the supernatural.

4

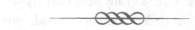

Before too long, Odalie Markette, inhabitant of Blois, became known as *L'animatrice*, the enabler. She had spirited on young men and women to become virtuosos in art, music, theater and voice. No one questioned Odalie's methods, her rules or her modus operandi. Parents and foster parents were interested in results performed in tests, on stage and at open recitals, and they paid handsomely for those results. However, once certain friendships and attachments became too close, Odalie would come up with some imagined illness or hardship which precluded her continuing with her student, and they were left on their own. Some continued and did well in their chosen field. Most became infatuated with other things and left their once-fascinating hobby at the foot of their beds. But the rumors of certain abilities to encourage success in others from associations with the interesting young woman from Blois spread throughout the region and all the way to the French Capital of Paris. And, Paris was listening close to such rumors.

Odalie had purchased her little cottage along the edge of the Loire River. Other such dwellings, their red-tile rooves glowing in the mid-day sun added to the charm of the century-old town. Clapboard sidings, all depicting medieval living conditions contributed to the atmosphere of a tourist location. Cobble-stone streets, little shops and a few bistro/restaurants completed the fairytale setting. But there was something else which lent itself to an already-attractive area---right next to Odalie's cottage was the Maison de la Magie Robert-Houdin, the museum dedicated to illusionism. On special occasions, the venue was also the site of performing arts presentations. In a big-lettered sign posted on the front of the museum, the next event read, 'Charles Dupont, Chanteur extraordinaire de Paris, le 2 octobre a 20 h'.

Odalie made sure that she had tickets for that performance. She loved the opera, and Charles Dupont was an up-and-coming opera star. The performance was only two weeks away, and Odalie made sure that she would be among theater goers that evening. Who knows, Monsieur Dupont might be looking for that fine edge which separates one professional from another. During the next two weeks, Odalie read and studied everything she could pertaining to how stage stars trained their voices, and she discovered some steps long forgotten by voice teachers throughout the country.

5

On the day before the recital, Charles Dupont had checked into the Hotel du Palais, the most exclusive and highly sought-after resting place in the city. He took dinner in the hotel's restaurant, met with some organizers of the musical event and asked questions about the town and its history. In the course of conversations, Odalie Markette's name was mentioned as being a person of some talent in helping young people reach their potential. Dupont inquired about Odalie's professional training, took note of what he had learned, and made a mental note of perhaps running into this talent scout. After all, picking up a few pointers and perfecting skills could not harm one's career in the business. He had asked members of his entourage to point Odalie out to him the night of the concert, and if possible, he would evaluate her ability to contribute to his success. Even those who knew nothing about opera singing might have stumbled on to a shortcut to stardom.

On the evening of the two-night engagement, the makeshift opera house of Blois was full of concert goers.

The mayor, his staff, all the city's leaders and their friends were taking their seats and readying themselves for a night of entertainment by the up-and-coming opera star from Paris, Charles Dupont. Gowns, tuxes, flowers, ushers, filled the auditorium, and ticket holders began to take their seats. Sitting in the first-row front, at the request of the star of the evening's performance, was Odalie Markette. She wore a sensuous red evening gown cut low enough to reveal an ample sampling of what was still covered but showed promise. Her dark hair was a well-prepared background for her facial beauty, and she was what most men would refer to as ravishing. Before the curtain was lifted, all eyes were on the woman who had a reputation for bringing out the best in people, but everyone wondered how such a beautiful woman could also be so prolific in both beauty and ability.

Days previous to the evening performance, Charles Dupont had requested that he meet the woman whose reputation was based on the development of a person's skills. He met with Odalie and was accompanied by city officials in Odalie's riverside cottage. Tea was served, and Dupont was mesmerized by a scintillating beauty and her supposed ability to finetune someone's special talent. When he asked Odalie how she might be able to help an opera singer improve his skills, she simply said, "If one were to look deep enough into what seemed to be a gift, they would find that there was always one or two things which needed polish. If those things were pointed out by someone not blinded by theater lighting, a revelation could take place." When Dupont asked whether Odalie would meet privately with him and under different lighting look deeply, she responded, "Anything is possible, but at the moment, I feel somewhat skittish in the presence of such a virtuoso. Time will tell." The stage was already in motion of being set.

6

On the opening of the curtain, Charles Dupont received a standing ovation. Once seated, with an accompanying orchestra, he sang the part of Rodolfo from *La Boheme*. His voice carried well to all parts of the theater. After an excellent rendition of his Alfredo from *La Traviata,* the audience accepted the fact that they might be seeing the next Luciano Pavarotti. But Dupont's next selection was directed to the beautiful young woman in the red dress in the front row of the auditorium. Walking up to the edge of the stage, Dupont started his presentation by pointing a finger at the ravishing young beauty in the first row. He then went into Verdi's, *La donna e mobile,* and all those who knew the story were sure that the reference to a woman's being dubious was directed to nonother than Odalie Markette.

At the end of the spectacle, much appreciated by all the attendees, Dupont received bouquets of flowers. Some theater goers were invited to his dressing room behind the stage, and among them was Odalie Markette. After a few obligatory embraces, and subtle comments, Dupont made his way to Odalie and said, "Eh, bien, mademoiselle, est-ce que vous pensez qu'il y a assez d'espace de perfection?" Knowing exactly that a contract was open for Odalie to ply her skills and improve upon excellence, she said, Monsieur Dupont, si vous acceptez mes regles, et si vous suivez mes suggestions, dans un mois, vous serez en haut du monde." The contract between the teacher and her pupil had just been verbally signed, and work would begin the next day in an effort to make the opera star even more competent and important in his quest to improve.

The very next day after the evening performance, Charles Dupont appeared at the door of Odalie's cottage, and he carried a bouquet of a dozen red roses. In a meeting arranged at the end of last evening's stage presentation, it was agreed that the singer and his new teacher/advisor would get together early. Odalie, decked out as usual in a beautiful and revealing rose-colored sundress, met her new pupil and they took seats at a table in the living room. Dupont made several references as to the attractiveness of his teacher, and Odalie got right to the point. She made it very clear that her suggestions for improvement would not be based on her knowledge of scale, pitch or voice range. Her recommendations would have to do with poise under stress, theatrical delivery and the ability to captivate audiences with the flair of a professional actor. Once that was understood, she moved on to another part of the agreement---personal accord between instructor and student.

In no uncertain terms, Odalie outlined the social and professional commitment which would take place between student and teacher. No reference to any personal or intimate association was to occur between the working partners of the agreement. Dupont pouted appropriately, and in spite of his being attracted to his appointed advisor, he agreed that no stepping across this agreed-upon line would occur. Odalie continued with her issuing a warning: should any intimacy be suggested by either party, or should the consent to enter into any close physical or romantic association take place, the consequences would result in the breaking of contract and might even lead to a decline in professional achievement of the pupil.

Dupont scoffed silently at what he thought to be a naivete of his young, unskilled instructor. After all, he had taken lovers from both the orchestra and the cast of most of his productions, and some of those liaisons still were in place. For the moment, he, the receptor of advice, would adhere to rules set in place. But he also know that fickleness existed outside Verdi's, *La donna e mobile*. Odalie was young, beautiful and vulnerable. He, Dupont, was, to most young women, irresistible, promising and available. And, in the weeks to come, he made it known to Odalie that to him, feminine company was not in any way lacking.

7

Between shows, Odalie prompted her student to pay attention to non-musical attributes. He, the singer, would practice voice enhancement, memorization of line, measure and timber while she, the enhancer, would focus on flair, theatrical presence and temperament. That collaboration produced a seasoned practitioner of the arts, and Charles Dupont soon became one of the most-called upon professionals to sing in one city after another. Odalie accompanied her protégé on every road trip, and separate rooms and beds were de rigueur in every venue. But, to Charles Dupont, his teacher's beauty still intrigued him. He could not dispel the urge to savor the beauty and voluptuousness of the woman who was making him a star.

Overtures had been made on more than several occasions, especially after a successful engagement, that a more intimate liaison be established. Dupont explained that, should he be allowed to taste what had been called to his attention, beauty, charm, that yet unclaimed thing, he would become an even better practitioner of his art. Odalie had resisted every suggestion of a more-serious arrangement; she knew and felt that her contract with her pupil was her bond. And, deep down, she also felt that any dalliance in their association could result in failure and collapse. But nature, as fickle as the female lead in Verdi's *La donna e mobile*, was to play its part. And, soon.

Two weeks after Dupont's successful performance in Blois, he received an invitation to appear at the fashionable and new opera center in Paris, The Opera Bastille, which had become the main facility of the Paris National Opera. The building seats over 2,700 music and ballet lovers, and it acts as a venue for experimental performances. Dupont was invited to take part in a combined opera/ballet production, and he accepted the invitation, but not before he implored Odalie Market to accompany him to Paris. Everything was arranged, and the opera singer and his advisor took the afternoon train from Blois and arrived in Paris early in the evening. The two people checked in their hotel, were given separate rooms, had dinner and retired for the evening.

Early the next morning, Dupont and his working partner took breakfast and spent the rest of the day discovering the new music venue in the Bastille. Arrangements were made for programs, private audiences were given the singer and his guest, and they were conducted through the enormous building. The singer spent time practicing his profession, and the woman who accompanied him did some shopping in and around the Bastille area. Two nights later, the performance took place as scheduled, and Charles Dupont was an instant hit in Paris. A dinner celebration was held at the Jules Verne Restaurant on the Eiffel Tower. Champagne flowed freely, and the musician and his lady companion returned to their hotel, and that is where either a mistake or a crucial decision was made.

Charles Dupont accompanied his partner, the beautiful Odalie Markette, to the door of her hotel room. The couple lingered there for a brief moment, and Dupont took that opportunity to draw her to his body, and he kissed her passionately on the lips. She did not resist his intentions, but she did say, "Charles, if you persist in your desire to make our association more than that upon which we agreed, you must be aware that any intimacy we share will more than likely end in disappointment for both of us." Dupont's reply was simple. "Odalie Markette, you are the most beautiful women I have ever known, and I want everything possible from you. I want your support. I want your company. I want your knowledge, and I want your body...now."

8

The next morning, the doors of the Hotel de l'Opera were swinging freely both ways, and it was not unusual to see well-dressed men and women frequenting the establishment at all hours of the day or night. But one such patron of the hotel, a young and very attractive woman was leaving the hotel with a small carrying case in hand. She wore a light-weight overcoat and rain hat. Even though covered by clothing, the young woman was able to elicit from men standing near the hotel the under-the-breath expression, "Bien tournee!" They knew a well-proportioned young woman when they saw one, and this young lady had everything in just the right places.

Odalie Markette was leaving the hotel and her exciting weekend behind. She had allowed the man whom she was coaching to invade her privacy, and her last night in the hotel was spent in the arms of a man who had passionately become her lover, something which would break the bonds of professionality agreed upon weeks earlier. She carried in and on her body the remanences of her lover's attentions brought on by uninterrupted hours of passion. She was satiated, her body spent, and she needed rest from the intensity of last night's allowances.

She took a taxi to the Gare d'Austerlitz, boarded the train for her hometown, Blois, and settled in at a window seat from which she said her goodbyes to Paris and to her former pupil's memory. Once the opera singer realized that he had broken a bond made solid by solemn vows, he would understand why he woke up alone in his hotel. Odalie, now seated in her window seat on the train, slipped on a faux wedding ring; she wanted no interlocutions from young bachelors or married men. Odalie was looking forward to her return to her little town's offer of less stress and strain. She ordered a cup of tea from the train's galley and slipped in a morning-after pill, and passed her time reading the ads from those who needed help in motivating themselves to do better.

The trip to Blois from Paris took less than two hours. As soon as Odalie arrived at her destination, she walked the short distance to her home and once again made herself busy with getting her little cottage in shape for the days to come. She answered no phone calls. She wanted a complete separation from the man she had helped regain his professional composure. She had completed her part of the bargain, and was prepared for further adventure wherever it might lead.

9

When Charles Dupont awoke the next morning, he found himself alone. He was not surprised when he realized that Odalie Markette had left his room. While she was a willing participant in last night's love making, she had hinted that such an act might have consequences. In spite of the fact that Odalie was one of the most beautiful women he had ever seen, he did know that his recent fame would draw women to him light a street light to moths. He prepared himself for the day, made ready to practice his trade and looked over upcoming concerts. He was self-assured that his career was on the upswing, and looked forward to whatever was to take place. And, that mental focus seemed to work for a while.

Dupont's next-scheduled performance was to take place in the St. Denis Cathedral just north of Paris. A full card of religious music was to be given, and he prepared himself for the concert to take place in a church which was the depository for the kings and queens of France since Clovis in the fifth century. The fact that he would find himself in such a coveted place did not worry him in the least; he was a trained professional, and practitioners of his trade did not worry.

On the evening of his performance, the cathedral was packed with music lovers, religious worshipers and attendees who wanted to see the latest star of vocal talent. The Overture to Les Miserables was played, and Charles Dupont stepped out on the stage and began his rendition of Jean Valjean at the barricades. At first, the audience thought that the singer might have been ill. He hesitated, and did not come in on cue, seemed to confuse his lines. Dupont recovered and went on, and his singing elicited huge applause from the audience. The next day, Paris newspapers accused last night's singer of being tired and overworked. However, repeated performances uncovered other musical and theatrical faux pas, and within a short time, further tours of Dupont's group were cancelled without explanation. Phone calls to Odalie's little cottage in Blois were unanswered. In less than six months, the career of Charles Dupont, a once up-and-coming singer of opera and other light pieces of music, was at a standstill, and could not be renewed. Dupont was last seen giving singing lessons to young men and women aspiring to be the next heartthrobs of the concert stage.

10

Speculation about the sudden collapse of Dupont's professional life began immediately. Everyone noticed that the beautiful woman who had been part of his entourage had suddenly disappeared from view. She was nowhere to be found, and when anyone inquired with hotel personnel in Paris, it was discovered that she had checked out the morning after Dupont's last Paris engagement. The inability to pin down what had happened to Odalie Markette did not prevent rumors to be spread. One report hinted that Dupont's one-time associate was his muse and that she alone controlled his musical talent. Others, more inclined to look into the occult, outlined specific rituals which led to Dupont's success. But, the stunningly beautiful Odalie Markette was nowhere to be found. There were other starlets who followed, and the fickleness of celebrity worshipers dictated that other such champions of entertainment could be found. Such deviations of public opinion suited Odalie just fine.

The beautiful young woman who had enhanced the career of an opera singer did not miss her association with the star of stage and theater. She was not without interested suiters. Like other attractive women her age, she did enjoy the amorous attentions of young men. But she had much yet to do in showing others the way to success. It was this *idee fixe* that motivated her to look for young people in need of that extra push, that *Je ne sais quoi* which sets them apart from others by their age and skill. She took out an ad in a local journal proclaiming the ability to help others in their quest to excel. Before long, one such mother, who could not afford professional piano teachers to help her daughter enjoy the instrument contacted Odalie at her home and inquired about what might be done for the daughter interested in playing the piano.

The teacher, the mother and her daughter met in Odalie's little cottage and discussed what it was that brought the mother and daughter to the cottage. The mother spoke first and said that she wanted her daughter to learn the basic techniques of playing the piano. Odalie listened, and then she looked at the daughter and said, "Mademoiselle, why are you interested in playing the piano? What do you hope to be able to do with such a skill?" The child looked up at the woman whom she hoped would be able to help her enjoy an instrument she knew little about and said, "The piano is such a beautiful thing. It should be allowed to talk to us." With a smile on her face, Odalie Markette said, "In one week's time, I will come to your home, and we will have a conversation with your friend, the piano."

The cost of instruction was established, days lessons would be conducted and outlined, and verbal agreements were made. The mother and Odalie's new pupil left the cottage, and the next few days were devoted to the ins and outs of learning how to become acquainted with the shortcuts to piano playing. And, Odalie did her research. She read anecdotes about world-renowned pianists and their practice habits.

In her search for information about piano virtuosos, Odalie knew that she was not going to teach music theory. Her pupil wanted to make her instrument talk. To her, the piano was a toy, a thing to be enjoyed, and she had no aspirations to become a concert pianist. That being said, the girl's teacher set about to discover what some famous pianists did which made them stand out in their profession. She looked into Chopin's use of melody and harmony. She read about Liszt and his use of virtuosic skills and magnetic charisma. She discovered that Rachmaninoff used his supreme technical agility and emotional intensity to enhance his playing. She also learned that Beethoven's deafness was overcome by a simple discovery---music is a language, with rules. Knowing the rules of how music is made can enhance skills at the piano. Odalie Markette studied these traits and put them into her lesson plans for the days and months to come. Then, she took time out for herself.

Having her lessons planned for the days ahead gave Odalie time to revisit and appreciate her own home town of Blois. She took time to explore the town's famous chateau where, in 1429, Joan of Arc was blessed by the Archbishop of Reims before she chased the English out of the near-by city of Orleans. The chateau contains 564 rooms with 100 bedrooms all of which contain their own fireplace. The chateau was the home of Charles d'Orleans, the famous poet who was captured by the English at Agincourt and held captive in the Tower of London. Odalie walked through the bedroom of Marie de Medici, the wife of Henri IV, and marveled at the furniture hundreds of years old and still in excellent shape. After her visit, Odalie took tea in a little shop opposite the chateau and prepared for her tutoring of a young girl fascinated with her family's piano.

Odalie's young student made remarkable progress during her first week's instruction. The student had been motivated by her teacher to practice the correct skills the right way, and in the process, develop a love for her instrument. The young girl was inspired by her new knowledge of Chopin's use of melody, and she was aware that physical setbacks such as Beethoven's poor hearing did not impair his ability to make beautiful sounding music. The girl's parents were astounded with their daughter's new interest in music, and they paid Odalie above what had been agreed upon. Odalie had what one might say was a magic touch in her ability to bring out excellence in her students. Soon, other parents of young children were imploring Odalie to take on new students, and she did.

11

Chantel, Odalie's newest piano protégé, drew the mother's attention immediately. "Madmoiselle Markette, ma fille ne guitte le piano pendant jour et nuit, et elle proclame que manger n'est plus necessaire." Odalie did not want to hear that one of her pupils was so enamored with her study and practice of music that she would give up eating in order to spend more time at the keyboard. Teacher and student talked about good health going hand in hand with professional excellence, and everything was resolved with Chantel's mother. But something else came to the teacher's attention.

Yes, all the scales necessary to piano playing were exhibited on demand, and they were played exceptionally well. Some of the most well-known classics were displayed for the teacher's benefit, but something was being held back. Chantel's mother divulged that her daughter had been playing something which sounded totally American and did not sound like classical music. An exhibition had been scheduled for the middle of next month, and student and teacher were planning a list of songs to be played. Days passed like they were winter's snows melting away in the warm spring sunshine. It was time, and a new season was emerging.

On the evening of the recital scheduled to take place in the Chateau de Blois's grand gallery, chairs were set up, and a grand piano was put in place. Verbal excitement gave proof of parental are family support to the candidates on the official roster. Teachers were given a special seating area, and the sponsor of the evening's event gave a very moving welcome to the audience and participants. And, then, the first contestant was called to the piano.

One after another, each participant was given the opportunity to play two short pieces followed by a longer version of a well-known composer's work. Chantel's turn was next to last, and her teacher began to wonder whether the wait would interfere with her being ready to perform. However, the expression on the face of Odalie's student gave evidence of complete confidence and control. The young girl's smile was added evidence of professional decorum and trust. Finally, it was Chantel's turn at the piano, and she walked up to the instrument with poise, sat down and started her first piece.

Chantel's first piece on her lineup was a short, watered-down version of Beethoven's 'Moonlight Sonata' which starts off with a slow progression and leads to a crescendo and powerful ending. Light applause greeted the end of Chantel's first effort. Her second piece came from Chopin's 'Nocturne in C-Sharp Minor', and in that rendition, the black and white keys of the piano produced a thing of beauty. Again, light applause greeted the young pianist. Then, Chantal got up from her seat, moved the piano stool out of the way and approached to piano standing. She stood over the keyboard and, as if she were attacking an on-coming shark in rough waters, began her rousing rendition of a piece of music by Jerry Lee Louis. Her interpretation of 'Whole Lot of Shakin' Going On', both vocal and piano, sent a spark into the audience who, to a person, rose and clapped along with the beat coming from the fingers and voice of a young, talented school gir from the City of Blois.

To say that Chantel's piano recital was a success would be an understatement. Her playing was superior to most other contestants, and the novelty of her choice of music pleased everyone in the audience. However, the judges, bathed in the classical tradition, could not allow one of their proteges to win such a prestigious competition. After all, awarding the first prize to a contestant who idolized a piano player nicknamed "The Killer", didn't set well with most people. Odalie's student, Chantel, took second prize, and the audience reacted with a very negative whistling at the judges' decision. Chantel's mother on the other hand, rewarded her daughter's teacher with a monetary gift and a request for a continued tutoring of what many considered an up-and-coming star. Odalie accepted her payment, but no agreement for further tutelage was made. Odalie Markette had made her mark.

12

In the days following the piano recital for up-and-coming starlets, Odalie busied herself with becoming more familiar with her town and her community. She had not been born in the city of Blois, but she loved exploring its nooks and crannies as if she were an explorer searching for new lands. Every day, she would discover some new aspect of her community. In doing so, she encountered a small tearoom close to her little cottage. She became friends with the owner, a woman Odalie's age, the two would have tea together on a regular basis. Her new friend, Monique Mayes, told Odalie about newcomers to the area, and one of them, a young American male, had just opened an antique shop close by. Odalie had studied English at the university, and she was eager to try out that language with an authentic American.

In less than a week after learning from Monique about the young American antique seller, Odalie decided to drop by and introduce herself to the owner. One sunny afternoon, after a shot stop at her favorite tearoom, she made her way to the newest shop in town. The antique shop was not hard to locate. In a three-centuries-old building, the antique shop was located on the first floor of a four-story edifice. On either side of the main entrance, two large picture windows displayed centuries-old farm implements, firearms and swords collected from ancient battlefields and nicknacks from households of the past. The building lent itself to the efforts of the shop owner. The old stone structure had preserved the feeling of the past, and an antique shop completed its rightful place in the community. Odalie stepped into the entrance way, pushed open the door to the store and was greeted by the ringing of a little bell suspended from the top of the door.

At first glance, Odalie believed that the little shop was either empty of working personnel or closed for the day. But emerging from a small office in the rear of the store was a young man Odalie's age who immediately welcomed her with, "Bonjour Mademoiselle. Bienvenue a 'Les Choses du Passe'. C'est le nom de mon entreprise ici a Blois." Odalie responded, "Pardon, Monsieur. On dit que vous etes American."

–   Oui, Mademoiselle. Je viens de l'etat de New York et de La Nouvelle Orleans.
–   Genial! Ca vous derange si l'on parle anglais?
–   Au contraire, Mademoiselle. That would please me very much. Names were exchanged and the first meeting of the two people continued.

Much to Odalie's liking, she, an English major at university, the rest of the dialog between the two acquaintances was in English. Odalie learned that the shop's owner, Vernon Sarvey, had served in the American military, gone to college and earned a degree in French history and literature. He had fallen in love with French culture and decided that by opening a shop of French antiques, he would become even more familiar with the past of that country. As he recounted his reasons for being in Blois, Odalie took a liking to this young man who admired her country, and at the same time, cautiously recommended to herself to curb any serious and more intimate relationships with her American.

As introductions and small talk continued, other common pieces of information were exchanged. Odalie expressed her liking for the way Vernon had arranged his antiques for display, and she commented on the authenticity of items shown. After voicing his appreciation of his visitor's admiration of things collected, Vernon took the next step in letting it be known that Odalie had ignited a spark in the fast-growing relationship, and he asked Odalie if she would be his guest for dinner on the coming Saturday evening. Without hesitation, Odalie answered, "Having the opportunity to improve my English would be a pleasure, Vernon. Now on a first-name basis, it was established that the dinner would take place at '*La Grenouillere*' a trendy restaurant not far from the Chateau de Blois. In his French dictionary, Vernon later learned that *La Grenouillere* was translated as 'Frog Pond'.

The Saturday-night dinner times were confirmed, Odalie said her goodbyes, and both the newly-met people had the distinct impression that something good would come from the chance acquaintance. Everyone likes old things, and the more time spent with them, a familiarity develops quickly.

Getting ready for their next meeting had both parties scurrying for outfits which would enhance chances of a lasting relationship. Odalie wanted this to happen as much as did Vernon Sarvey. Both people were young, attractive, and they liked the company of the opposite sex. To Vernon, Odalie, was a dream come true. Young, beautiful, intelligent, and she spoke English which would help him perhaps meet others who had similar interests. For Odalie, she had not had any romantic association since she left her opera singer in Paris. The time seemed just right for an experiment to take place which might just lead to a reward for both parties.

La Grenouilliere Restaurant was located close to the Loire River not far from the town's chateau and close to Odalie's little chalet. It was at one time in the past an old flower mill complete with a water-powered wheel which turned a large stone grinding surface. That had been removed to allow room for well-appointed booths for two or more diners. Between these booths, individual tables of old French oak allowed seating for groups of four to six. Old-style gas lights had been converted to electric use, and the décor was perfect for casual and more-intimate dining. Vernon had picked up his dinner companion, and as they entered the restaurant, they both agreed that the dinner place had been well picked.

For the rest of the evening, separated only by a candle at their table, stories about events in their youth, schooling, and travel were traded while a bottle of a nice lightly chilled

Sancerre from the Loire Valley promptly released any pent-up inhibitions between the two people at their table. The food, was very much French, and the *specialite de la maison* was *cuisses de grenouille au beurre.* No one, not even the American said that the frog legs tasted like chicken. Two hours later, both the American and the French woman arrived at Odalie's cottage door. Cautiously, Vernon said his goodnights, kissed Odalie on both cheeks and was about to walk away when, the woman who had been French kissed said, "C'est tout?"

Let it please the reader to know that an invitation to continue the evening may be verbal, visual and certainly sensual. In that order, and within the next three hours, that and more took place. Vernon became aware of how a woman's clothing covered and revealed at the same time. He learned that certain garments when allowed to slide over a woman's body, produced a quivering as well as an invitation. Vernon savored both the sensation and the offer. Exploration, discovery, surprise, exaltation and surrender took place off and on during the night. Both partners, now drained of exchange of passions, were lying side by side searching the ceiling of Odalie's bedroom for the answer to this adventure. Without looking at the woman to whom he had just made love, several times, Vernon said, "What just happened?" Odalie's very-fatigued reply was, *"Je ne sais pas. Mais, ca m'a beaucoup plu. "*

13

After their weekend awakening, the realization that something good, arousing and new had taken place, both Vernon and Odalie returned to their separate living areas. Odalie attended church at the local cathedral located near the chateau, and Vernon used his time to tidy up his antique shop for the coming week where, with a renewed enthusiasm, he hoped for increased interest in his curiosities on display. He spent some time recalling his hours with a beautiful creature he had just met, and he knew that he would see her soon. Such encounters were destined to continue over and over. Odalie's passion had been awakened, too, and she looked forward to seeing Vernon again. In her free time, she questioned whether she might in some small way enhance what he offered to the public. Could she, with her knowledge of the history and customs of France, somehow bring customers to the door of his little shop. She knew that she had that certain something which spurred into action someone willing to improve his or her way of enjoying life. And, that was how she came up with an idea to continue her association with a man who had awakened her passion for pleasure and company. She would propose an antique hunt to take place in and around the area of the Loire Valley, an historically rich center of culture past and present.

That Odalie was a little smitten with her new acquaintance was evident. She took special care in making herself presentable everywhere she went. Her clothing was chosen to show off form and elegance, and her smiles to everyone she encountered were genuine. She had become not only available, but sought after. Several single and some married men at her church had flirted and suggested a closer attachment. She offered no invitation to continued attention. She was now focused on forming a relationship, not especially sexual but social with the new antique dealer in town. Should anything further develop with that situation, Odalie was open to it. Vernon had already proved to be a passionate and knowledgeable lover, and if that were to continue, so be it. That she had once thought that romance would terminate relationships was a thing of the past. But it was Odalie's intention to offer some advice to her new friend. And besides, she liked delving into and learning more about the past.

Within a week after their first dinner outing, Odalie arrived at the door of Vernon's shop, pushed in the door and entered his establishment. The smile on Vernon's face gave away his emotions. He was delighted to see the most beautiful woman in Blois enter his store. If such a person showed interest in what he had to sell, others would make an effort to see what had attracted the most sought-after beauty in town. "Good morning, Mr. Antique dealer. Tell me what is old and interesting."

"Mademoiselle, let me talk first of what is young and beautiful, a genuine citizen of Blois who knows more about this country than I."

"Well stated, Mr. Sarvey. Would you be interested in taking a little trip to some of the small towns in this area to scout out new discoveries?"

"What a splendid idea. I could not have thought of anything better. You could be my official authenticator on things found and of value to those who treasure the past. When could we start?"

"Do you have days when your shop is closed? We could rent a car and visit some of the little roadside displays and little curio shops in the area. There are more than several of them in our region."

"Monday is my slow day, and that would give me the time to see what could be added to my collection. And, by the way, I have a little car, and I am a licensed driver here in France. Would next Monday suit you, Mademoiselle Markette?"

"Vernon, please call me Odalie. The closeness of these past few days justifies that, and I would love to show you around the area. I, too, love things from the past, and discovery is exciting."

"Odalie, I would agree on that. The discoveries I have made just this past weekend have more than wetted my appetite for further exploration. Should we meet before next Monday and plan our outing."

"No, Vernon. Let me look into what might be available. I will meet you here next Monday bright and early. Say 9 A.M."

"Perfect. And, until then…?"

"We both have some work to do. I cannot wait."

"Odalie, you have no idea. Let time pass quickly."

Mademoiselle Markette made her way home, and she was proud of herself; she had not thrown herself at her recent lover's feet, and she wanted to know what might be next. She had only a short time to wait, and she needed to make some new discoveries with this young American.

14

In the days leading up to the outing hunting for antiques, Odalie busied herself looking into areas close to Blois where little shops might prove valuable in the search for old things discarded and forgotten. She located one such place not far from Blois located west of the town and close to the Loire River. In the early 1400's the most famous French poet of the fifteenth century, Francois Villon, had been imprisoned in a hole in the ground in the town of Meung-sur-Loire. The poet, a murderer, criminal and gang member had been incarcerated for public disorderly conduct, and was released when a French king passed through the town. His collection of poems included his *Grand Testament* and *Petit Testament* in which he wrote some of the most memorable lines of all time such as "But where are the snows of yesteryear?", and "I am dying of thirst at the foot of the fountain." One of his poems, now lost, was entitled, 'The Romance of the Devil's Fart', which, in French was *'Le Pet au Diable'*. The title so intrigued Odalie, she researched the poem and learned more about the wayward poet.

Finding research material on Francois Villon anywhere in the world and on-line is not difficult; writers, researchers, college professors and their students have tried to pin down what might have enabled the one-time murderer and criminal to become the best-known poet of the fifteenth century. Odalie had studied his poetry in university, and she knew much about his meanderings through France. One of the stops on next Monday's outing with Vernon Sarvey would be the little town of Meung-sur-Loire, not far from Blois, and she was almost sure that antique shops would be plentiful in such an old and once-important city.

Europeans and especially the French loved things from the past. Unlike the Americans who, on occasion, erase vestiges of their past, the French are proud of those who lived, worked and achieved throughout history. In Paris at *Le Marche au Puce,* antique hunters can find almost something from the last two thousand years. But Odalie and her new friend, Vernon, would restrict their search to the immediate area of the Loire Valley. While Odalie was mapping out a probable route for next Monday's search, she did wonder where her new friendship might lead. She liked this young American. He was well-mannered, spoke French, and the one time she had allowed him to make love to her, he proved to be …on top of things, and she liked his positioning skills. But enough of that; she had work to do.

Maps were visited, directions confirmed and curio shops and antique dealers in the Loire Valley were noted. For some reason, perhaps because of her success in helping others achieve their dreams, she had a good feeling about what her American friend might accomplish. France was rich in vestiges from the past. Many had already seen the light of day in that discovery, but there is always something overlooked because of lack of knowledge and research. Odalie's spirits about her trip and about her new friend were lifted. She was ready for something new, whatever that entailed.

15

When Vernon pulled up in front of Odalie's little cottage early Monday morning, he did not expect to be greeted by his traveling companion in a beautiful sundress. Odalie looked stunning, and she carried a picnic basket which would provide lunch and thirst-quenchers along the way. Customary kisses were traded, greetings voiced, and within minutes, Vernon and his fellow antique hunter were on their way west of the city keeping the Loire River on the driver's side of the road. People going to their work and businesses filled the highway, but by 9:30 A.M., the roads had cleared and offered a clear view of both sides of the thoroughfare. Vernon asked where the first stop might be, and Odalie said, "Do you know anything about Francois Villon and his stay in prison in Meung-sur-Loire." Vernon gave a resume of what the 15 th century poet had done to be condemned to be placed in the criminal pit at Meung, how he had regained his freedom, and his association with the noble, Charles d'Orleans in the mid 1500's.

Odalie was pleased with Vernon's knowledge, and she explained that Meung would be their first stop along the way. She told him of a little curio shop off the beaten path which had a reputation of having acquired things of interest. Personal items of those who lived centuries ago would have been scattered or buried with the deceased, but one never knew. An hour later, the antique hunters pulled into the outskirts of the little town of Meung.

At first sight, the little town of Meung does not attract the newcomer. Large fields of grain-producing vegetation, colorful flowers growing roadside, and trees obstructing the view of the first buildings which come into view. The long viaduct bridge, now in shambles cluttered the main stream flowing through the area. At the beginning of the German invasion in 1940, French partisans blew up the bridge before the Germans arrived, and its wreckage does not add beauty to the little community. As you get closer to the center of town, stone buildings dating several centuries old portray a more-welcoming view. Some of the ancient structures were made into restaurants, bistros, wine shops and flower stalls, and those structures had drawn tourists from other parts of France.

George Simenon's classic fiction character, Maigret, retired in Meung-sur-Loire, and some very gullible tourists aways looked for his residence. The Chateau de Meung was used as a prison, and in the mid-15th century, its dungeon was the place of captivity for Francois Villon who had escaped punishment in Paris. The Chateau is one of today's tourist attractions, and visitors still ask if Villon left anything behind.

On the outskirts of the town center, a few good-looking restaurants showed evidence of good cuisine; outdoor tables were full, and right next to the well-attended eateries was an antique shop. Its façade gave evidence of several centuries old mason work. Glass windows on both sides of the large main door displayed things discarded centuries ago but made attractive to a newer generation. Odalie and Vern were immediately drawn to the little shop, but both decided that lunch might be best before any exploration took place. Before too long, the couple had a table, ordered a light meal and observed other luncheon guests around them.

16

Restroom calls were made, bills paid, and the antique seekers were on their way to the store now open just doors away. The building which contained the relics from the past was itself, a thing from the years gone by. As Odalie and Vernon stepped up to the door of the establishment, it was as if a portal to the past was open to them. Centuries of soot, accumulated street dust and time itself had painted the little shop a thing seen in tourist photos or photo albums kept over the years. The couple pushed open the main door, and they entered into a depository of things collected over the centuries. The proprietor, an old man wearing spectacles that Voltaire might have worn in the eighteenth century greeted Odalie with a "Mademoiselle" and a nod. He introduced himself as Paul Vauclud, owner. Vernon's presence seemed to be not that important. Even old men past their prime cannot avoid showing preference to beautiful woman. Odalie and the antique seller exchanged greetings and it was explained that a young American had come to France with the idea of dabbling in the purchase and sale of antiques. Only then was Vernon's presence acknowledged. The antique owner told Odalie and Vernon to look at anything they liked, and if they had questions, he would be available.

Vernon mentioned the name, 'Brocante', which was painted on the main window of the shop. He knew that the word was related to antiques but wondered what else it might mean. Odalie explained that the word usually referred to a flea market where everything, clothing, furniture, toys, maps and postcards could be had.

"Vernon, have you ever been to Les Puces de Saint Ouen in Paris?"

"I have heard about it, but I have never been there."

"You could spend days there. It's the largest antique market in the world, and if you have an item you're searching for, it's there."

"Maybe you and I could spend a weekend there… together."

Odalie did not respond to Vernon's suggestion, but her smile betrayed her thoughts, and she began to ask herself where this liaison was headed. For the next hour, Odalie and her American friend made their way through the stacks of items collected over the years. Vernon found some farm tools dating back a hundred years, and he picked out what might have been a blacksmith's pair of plyers. Just as the couple were making their way toward the exit of the shop, Vernon caught sight of a piece of board which measured about 3' by 4', and from the looks of it, it had been cut from one solid tree trunk years and years ago. The thing the intrigued him the most was a cut-out design in one corner of the large board which looked like a barbed tail. I had been at one time in the past tinted red but only a slight stain existed now. Alone side the image were the words, 'Le Pet au Diable'. He drew Odalie's attention to the drawing and the words on the panel.

Odalie took a closer look and hesitated for almost a minute. Then, she took Vernon's arm and quietly escorted him toward the door. She said her goodbyes to the shop owner. Vernon did the same, and Odalie looked at Vernon and whispered, "Don't point or make reference to that board until we get back to a café or to a hotel. I will explain later."

17

Once they had exited the antique store, Odalie took Vernon's hand and said, "We need to discuss something." By this time, Vernon, still struck by the beauty of the young woman beside him, said, "Odalie what's going on?"

"Let's order a cup of tea at the shop across the street. I need to tell you a little story." Vernon put up no struggle. Tea sounded good, and he was ready and willing to listen to whatever his new friend had to say.

"Vernon, how much do you know about Francois Villon?"

"Well, in my graduate studies, all of us had enrolled in a course on Villon's works. We read *Le Petin Testament, Le Grand Testament* and just about everything the poet wrote. We studied excerpts from his life, and most of us became devotees to his work."

"That's good. Do you know that one of his poems was never found or recorded?"

"None of us were aware that anything else had been written."

"Well, my young American friend, it is rumored that one poem, a piece written about him and his friends playing tricks on the owner of a drinking establishment in Paris has never been recovered."

"My fellow students and I were not aware of that story."

"One of my professors at the University of Grenoble told me and others in the class that Villon and his cohorts would steal pub signs from establishments and hold them for ransom. The signs would carry the name of the drinking place, and they were worded so as to inspire interest in passers-by. Signs such as 'Le Chat Qui Dort.' 'Le Chien Qui Parle.', and so on were popular. Those signs were usually stamped out on blocks of wood and hung near the door of the drinking place. They were the neon signs of the 15th century, and they were worth some money. Villon and his fellow thieves would steal these signs and charge the owners for their return."

"Now, that, Odalie is interesting. You have contributed to my knowledge of Francois Villon. Thank you. But why did we leave the antique shop so abruptly?"

"Do you remember passing by the large piece of board just inside the antique shop?"

"Yes, what about it?"

"Did you see what the sign board said?"

"Not really, but there was a symbol carved out which looked like a barbed tail."

"Did you notice the words cut out on the board?"

"No, I thought my arm was going to be pulled out of joint when you dragged me out of the shop."

"Vern, the words on the sign were, 'Le Pet au Diable', the Devil's fart. That was one of the pubs in Paris during the 15 century and that was the title of Villon's last uncovered poem."

"Wait a minute, Odalie. Are you saying that the big piece of wood we saw might be something stolen by the poet and his gang in the 15ᵗʰ century? It would have to be over five-hundred years old."

"Mon ami, Vern, we are in France. Our country has been around for more than two-thousand years. And, if that big piece of wood and its message could be carbon dated, and if it ended up in your shop, you, Monsieur, would not need a neon sign to advertise your business."

"What would you suggest, Miss French history teacher?"

"Let's sleep on it, and return tomorrow and inquire about using that piece of wood as a table top."

"Sleep on it?"

"Yes, it is too far to return to Blois and come back tomorrow. We could get a couple rooms and stay here for the night."

"A couple rooms? What if we were offered one room with one bed?"

"*C'est la vie,* life could be good."

That evening, a small local hotel did have one room with one bed. A young American man and a young French woman enjoyed the good life several times and woke up tired the next morning. Things were heating up for Odalie Markette, and she had decisions to make.

18

The following morning at breakfast with a croissant and café au lait, Vernon quizzed Odalie about the possibility of the block of wood they had seen in the *brocante* next door. "Odalie, might it be possible that that sign board could have been transported from Paris to the Loire Valley by the poet, Villon?"

"Knowing the antics of his actions, anything might be possible. He could have transported the thing with him during his travels hoping to sell it along the way. We don't know. However, I am not sure the owner of the antique shop is aware of the history of the poet. His work is studied in every French school, but not every student or citizen knows everything about the poet's meanderings."

"What do you suggest?"

"Vern, we could inquire with the shop's owner. However, we should not divulge everything we know. We could return to the antique dealer asking him if some small table might be available for a couple just starting out their lives together."

"A couple?"

"Just listen, Vern. We could browse around the store, settle on no individual piece and suggest that a large piece of wood could be made into a small table. For example, a nice piece of oak about 3' x 4'. Something similar to the piece of wood we noticed as we were exiting the shop. We could say that any marks on the block could be sanded away and made into what...a couple might need for a table top. Or, we could do the right thing; We could rid ourselves of any fraudulent guilt by simply asking the shop owner what he knows about the piece of wood he has. We have no idea of its origin, provenance or reason for its being among things for sale. Both of us would feel better if we just said that the piece caught our eye and that we found it interesting."

"Odalie, that idea appeals to me. I love the way you think, and it tells me a lot about what kind of a person you are."

"Vern, I am glad to hear you say that. Both of us will feel better about ourselves later."

"Feeling good about you, Odalie, is no problem where I am concerned."

"Why, Vernon Sarvey, you rascal, you."

"*Moi,* the rascal? You, *Mademoiselle,* take my breath away…like you did several times last night."

"Vern, I hope that was not a mistake. Our room had only one bed, and sleep is important."

"Why didn't I get any then? Sleep, that is."

"Stop. We must get ready and return to that shop and express our interest. Depending on the price of the piece, it would still look good in your shop window."

After a nice outdoor lunch, the two young antique seekers returned to the antique shop and questioned its owner about the interesting sign board he had. The antique dealer told Odalie and her escort that he had found the piece of wood in an old barn when he was looking for items for his shop. The barn's owner was cleaning things out in preparation for a sale of his farm, and he got rid of it cheap. But the new owner, the antique dealer, suggested that the piece might have been used to draw attention to a private residence although he wondered why the inscription was appropriate to a family's home.

Vern spoke up and said, "The inscription was the thing which drew my attention. These days, people's social mores were not as stringent as they had been in the past." The shop owner laughed and agreed that more than one person had questioned his reasoning on displaying such a thing and answered, "Do you want it?" Odalie said, "That might depend on the price, but it is an interesting object. What might be the price?" Without any hesitation, Monsieur

Vauclud, the shop owner said, "Thirty euros and it's yours if you take it today." Vernon countered with, "Twenty!", and Vauclud accepted immediately.

Both Vern and Odalie agreed on the price, and they added another five euros to the owner's request. A few minutes later, the big piece of sign board was loaded into their automobile, and the couple headed back to Blois. Odalie turned to her driver and said, "Vern, if nothing else, we did not take advantage of the seller, and you might want to change the name of your shop."

"Odalie, my love, let's do some research first."

"My love?', Vern?"

"Oops. Slip of the tongue. I'm sorry. I am just excited."

"Me, too. Now!"

19

Upon their return to Blois, the couple spent the night in their own homes and in their own bed. The block of wood with the interesting inscription was placed in Vernon's antique shop in one of his back rooms. Further investigation into the age, history and background of the big addition to Vern's collection would take place in the days to come, and the discovery of what both Odalie and Vern would find was going to prove more interesting than they had imagined.

Over the next few days, Vernon's phone calls to Odalie went unanswered, and that left the young American wondering where his liaison with Ms. Marquette was headed. Vernon liked the young woman he had just met. She was not only beautiful, she did not spurn his advances, and she reciprocated physically and emotionally with equal verve. Vernon Sarvey wanted more of this fascinating person. He hoped that she felt the same. As if his prayers had been heard, his phone rang, and he answered immediately. "Odalie?"

"Good afternoon, Vern. I have some news for you."

"I hope the news concerns your wanting to get together soon."

"That and more. We live in department of Centre-Val-de-Loire, and Blois is the capital city of the Loir-et-Cher department. As such, any requests for carbon dating of material is done right here in town."

"Odalie, that is perfect. What do we have to do?"

"This is what you must do. From your block of wood, making sure it is an integral part of the board, a sliver from that board will be needed for testing. I suggest you take that sliver from the back of the board."

"I can do that. Then, what?"

"Bring it to me here at home, and we will make plans to have that piece tested for an approximate date."

"How about dinner at the little bistro next to your home?"

"I would be available around 19:00. How's that?"

"That is perfect. It will be good to see you again."

"Likewise, Vern. Knock on wood."

Vernon went to work immediately on getting a small sample of wood from the back of his board. He then prepared himself for his get together with the woman whose mind and body had started to control…the rest of his body. For some reason, wooden blocks with inscriptions on them took second place as far as interest went in Vernon's mind. Inanimate objects took a far-off second when compared the voluptuous body of the woman whom he had just met.

20

Vernon was very careful in his selection of the sliver of wood from his newly-purchased sign board. He diligently stripped a small piece of the block and deposited it in a plastic sandwich bag. He then showered, shaved, and dressed for his meeting with the woman who would help him determine the age of his newly-acquired object of interest. Whether it was old or new, the block of wood and its inscription did stir the imagination, and it offered a valid reason to continue his opportunities to see the most beautiful woman in Blois.

Dinner at a trendy French restaurant near Odalie's home started and ended well. French cuisine is already well known by local citizen and tourists, and the weather offered out-door seating. Odalie wore a beautiful low-cut sundress, comfortable shoes, and she had applied what she thought to be enough makeup to appeal to any male passerby. But she did have very positive vibes for her young American lover. A bottle of Sancerre wine from the Loire Valley added to the warm summer breeze, and once they had settled down for dinner, the mention of the wood-block sliver came up.

"Vern, any problem coming up with an appropriate sample of your block of wood?"

"Odalie, let's call it our block of wood. Without your help, we would never have stumbled across such a piece. And, even it it proves to be a chunk of some tree grown last year, I will hold it as a token of our outing together."

"Vern, that is a lovely thought. Could I stop in your shop from time to time to look over our find?"

"Odalie, the door to my shop is always open to you and to anything you might suggest."

"*Genial!* Tomorrow, if you like, I could take our sample to the Municipal Building and inquire about our chances for carbon dating."

"I leave everything in your hands. But would it not be interesting if it were proven to be 15th century? If it does, what do we do?"

"Conduct a séance and entice a famous poet to tell us his story about what might have been one of the items he and his gang of thieves ripped off from some mediaval drinking establishment."

The rest of the evening was enjoyed to the hilt, and that is how far Vern's efforts led him that same night in Odalie's bed. But both Vern and Odalie had business of their own the next day, and that started early for both parties. The next morning, both Vern and Odalie attended to business. Vern brushed up and cleaned his newly-acquired artifact, and Odalie took the sample of wood Vern had given her to the science department of the local municipal building. There, she was told that the sample she had would be enough to determine its date, and that the entire process would take about a month.

Odalie had some decisions to make. She had done well working with others by helping them achieve their goals, but she did wonder about what the future might bring with her young American lover. She was still young and had attracted other suiters, but she shied away from any long or short-term relationships. Men about town, shop owners, provincial office holders and some married men had already suggested relationships. But Blois was a small town, and gossip was a non-discriminating predator; everyone was a target. And, small towns needed and thrived on juicy tidbits of information concerning citizens who thought themselves above reproach. Odalie liked her little town, and she was not going to jeopardize her standing which she had already established. In the days to come, Odalie was very reserved in her temptation to contact her newly-made friend from America.

21

The newest business in town, the little antique shop operated by a non-French national, drew interest. Vern had filled his *brocante*, his little flea market, with all sorts of bric-a-brac picked up at abandoned sites, road-side markets and on-line sales. Some of his best customers were American tourists who wondered into his shop as they visited the local chateaux and cathedrals. Taking things back home as souvenirs from their travel was provenance of having been there. And, yes, he did pine for further attachment to his beautiful French friend. Male ego and sexual prowess and passion do things to young men. It lets them know that life is worth living and a thing to be enjoyed.

Odalie, on the other hand, being a well-known member of her community, had an obligation to expected respectability; taking the arm of any and all suiters in town did not reflect well, and public opinion was mercurial; turning down the invitation from the wrong young man could prevent a rise in the respect shown at the market and places of business in town. In spite of her feelings for her young American friend, she was still French and, for the most part, followed the traditions set years before. She was reserved in her choice of friends.

One businessman in town, thought to be a respectable leader in the community, was not only the president of a local bank, he owned property in a few apartment complexes. One sunny afternoon as Odalie was taking tea at her favorite little bistro, Alexandre Martin, the bank president, entered the shop and approached Odalie's table. A man about fifty-years of age, neatly dressed, poised and ready for the world, came close to Odalie and stopped. He politely excused himself and asked if he might join her for a cup of tea.

"Mais, bien sur, Monsieur. Est-ce que je vous connais?" In response, the bank president said, "No, Mademoiselle, but I did hear that you also spoke English, and in my business, that is important. I also heard that you have an ability to enhance one's skills in almost any area of expertise. Let me introduce myself. My name is Alexandre Martin."

"Yes, Monsieur Martin. I am aware of who you are. Good afternoon. My name is Odalie Markette, and I live close by your establishment here in Blois."

"Would you mind if we continued our conversation in English?"

"Not at all, Monsieur Martin. We already are. I need practice, too."

The chance meeting with the bank president continued for another twenty minutes. After pleasantries were exchanged by both parties, Alexandre Martin excused himself and asked if he might call on Odalie at her home on occasion. Keeping a promise to herself, and perhaps thinking about antiques and new friends, Odalie said, "Monsieur Martin, I rarely entertain at home, and with a few exceptions, I do not invite males to visit me where I live. I am sure we will meet again, and if we do, our conversations in English will continue." Alexander Martin, shook Odalie's hand, did a small bow and walked away smiling thinking that he had opened a door which might have remained closed to him.

Weeks passed, and Odalie received several phone calls from Vernon Sarvey. He was interested in knowing whether she had heard from the Departmental Office in charge of carbon dating. To his delight, she said that she had. Vernon asked if they could have dinner the very next Saturday and discuss the findings. A date was set, and both would meet each other at the restaurant. Vernon did suggest that he could stop by her home on the way to the restaurant, but Odalie held fast to her request. She had decided to do more research into everything going on around her at the moment.

22

On the night of the dinner together at an upscale restaurant near Odalie's cottage, Vernon arrived early, sat himself at his table and awaited his date. Odalie arrived shortly after, and she was, as usual, the most beautiful woman in the restaurant. Vernon rose from his table, kissed Odalie on both cheeks, a new French custom he had practiced and commented on how stunning Odalie looked. Both shook hands and expressed how good it was to see each other.

Minutes after Odalie's arrival, a man and woman entered the restaurant together. Dressed in a very elegant manner, the couple checked in with the maître-D and were escorted to their table not far from Vern and Odalie. As they passed, the man stopped by Odalie's table, and with a surprise look on his face, he said, *"Bonsoir, Mademoiselle Markette. C'est un plaisir de vous revoir. Permettez-moi de vous presenter Madame Martin, ma femme."* Odalie greeted Alexandre's wife with a smile, and expressed her politeness in French. She then turned to Vern and said, *"Je vous presente Monsieur Vernon Sarvey, mon fiancé."* Everyone shook hands, and the bank president and his wife continued on to their table and took their seats.

"Odalie, my French is not as good as yours, but did I understand correctly that you referred to me as your fiancé?"

"Vern, your French is as good as mine. You don't miss a trick, do you. Let me explain." Odalie related that the bank president had encountered her a few days ago in her favorite tea room and had suggested that he stop by her home to say hello sometime in the future. Odalie also suggested that the man said nothing about his being married.

"That is amazing. I have heard stories about a Frenchman's roving eye, but to see it up close, that is interesting. Mr. Martin's wife didn't bat an eye the whole time."

"Vern, if you ever need a bank loan, let me go with you. I can almost assure you the Mr. Martin would have no objection to your request, and he is not going to want his wife to know that his interest lies elsewhere. However, something tells me that she knows a lot about her husband."

"Odalie, you are probably right. Now, let's get back to the word, '*fiance.*'" At that same time, the restaurant waiter arrived at Vern's table, and the dinner party began. Vern Sarvey had much to discuss with the most beautiful girl in town, and he was determined to not let it drop. But he was going to enjoy the verbal faux pas and milk it for all it was worth.

A nice bouillabaisse made with four different fish was ordered by both Odalie and Vern. One of the fish chosen was fresh trout from the Loire River just outside the restaurant. A good Sancerre, a white wine which complemented the bouillabaisse, was chosen by the wine steward, and during the meal, nothing more was said about the choice of words earlier. At the end of the meal, over coffee, Odalie said, "Vern, now is the time for us to discuss the results of our carbon dating from the wooden sign we picked up in Meung-sur-Loire."

"Odalie, that is at least one of the things on my mind. What have we learned?"

"The good news is this: that block of wood dates from the beginning to the middle of the 15th century. Its provenance suggests many things. There is no way we can deduce when the wording on the piece was inscribed, but a lot can be stated by supposition."

"In other words, one might say that the piece might have played a part in Vilion's life. Would that be responsible on our part?"

"Who's to say, Vern. But if you were to put the piece in your shop window and invite the opinion of the passerby or someone in search of something from the past, that could cause a stir in the community."

"I agree. We must say, of course, that there is not solid evidence that the sign board ever was hung in Paris or that the greatest poet and avowed criminal of the 15-century ever handled the piece. But public opinion, whether good or bad, is powerful."

"Norm, I will let you decide how the piece is to be displayed and how its rather unclear history should be handled. But if you are interested, we could work on it together."

"Well, someone dropped a hint about betrothal earlier. Togetherness seems to back that up."

"Vernon Sarvey, you know perfectly well why that word was used. I was protecting my reputation and my status as an unmarried young woman in town."

"I know, I know. I'm just having fun with that beautiful, unmarried young woman. Don't let me say any more. Let me walk you home."

And, that is exactly what they did. For the next two hours, in Odalie's second-floor bedroom, many things were discussed verbally, orally and passionately. Vernon arrived at his shop early in the morning, and he was happy. Togetherness is a wonderful thing.

23

Vern pondered over the right or wrong way to introduce his new piece to the public. Scamming the public for profit, especially in his new adopted country, was not in the cards. He liked Blois. He had become attracted to one of the most beautiful women he had ever known, and he knew that her values paralleled his own. But he also knew that the block of wood now in his store window had character. It was old, and the inscription on its surface and barbed tail showed promise of inspiring some collector of antiques. He decided to confide with Odalie on how one might bring attention to the sign board or whatever it was. And, he did have time.

Similar thoughts entered Odalie's mind. She had initiated the search for such a thing. She had researched the 15th-century poet's life and work, and thought that there just might be a chance that Villon and his cohorts might have removed evidence of their theft from Paris to Meung-sur-Loire. One thing for sure was the fact that the probability of proof, one way or the other, was undeniably out of the question; time and space had erased all traces of truth. It was now up to Vern. Maybe the two of them could transform a piece of old oak into a modern, sought-after relic. Stranger things had been done. And, working together with Vern was not such a bad thing. It had been exciting in so many ways.

Odalie Markette had accumulated a nice amount of reserve money with her assisting others to reach their potential. This new venture, helping a young American bolster his new business, was exciting, and his company had been both passionate and very intimate. She was enjoying the attention and its sidebar activities. She did wonder whether she should ask whether Vernon would like an active partner in his business, but she could not yet see a way of initiating such a move. She knew that it was coming, and she thought over how that subject might be proposed.

In the next few days, she went about her business, doing her almost daily marketing, stopping in for tea with Monique, the tea room owner. Odalie and Monique hit it off very well together. They were both the same age, single, both very attractive women, and they seemed to like similar things. Monique had heard and learned about Odalie's new American friend, and she decided one day to learn more. Over a few cups of tea, Monique inquired, "Well, Mlle Markette, is it still Mlle or has a closer union yet developed?"

"Monique, you inquisitive thing, you. Monsieur Sarvey and I are close friends. That's all. But something new has developed."

"Ah, ha, I knew it. You are engaged."

"No, silly. Listen. Vernon and I stumbled upon an old block of wood which, at one time in the past, was a sign board for some kind of establishment. Either a drinking place, small hotel or a shop of some kind."

"Can you describe this block of wood to me?"

"Certainly. It is about 3' by 4', and inscribed on its surface is an image of a barbed tail of some animal or… worse. The inscription carved into the wood says, '*Le pet au Diable.*'"

"Wait a minute. I am inclined to never use such language, but I do know what it means. 'The Devil's fart.' And, that is funny."

"Monique, that is not all, Vern and I had a carbon dating done on the piece, and it dates back to the 15th-century. But there is more. The greatest poet from that period of time, Francois Villon, wrote a poem using the same phrase, and the poem has never been found. Mention of its being written are in the journals of a criminal prosecutor in Paris; Villon was prone to criminal activity from time to time. What do you think of that?"

"Odalie, I think that you and your young American could do something with that piece of wood."

"Monique, Vernon is not 'my young American'. He's just a friend."

"Of course. And the Loire River does not hold water. I want to hear more about your friend and his piece of wood or whatever you call it these days.

"Monique, I love you, but that was not funny."

Odalie's laughter brough stares from fellow tea drinkers.

A few more friendly insinuations were exchanged, and Odalie did drop a hint that the relationship between her and Vern Sarvey sometimes involved close personal encounters which were not fully disclosed. And for that reason alone, the young shop owner embellished her own and more-touching story of her friend and the young American.

24

Just about the moment when Odalie got up from her table and proceeded toward the shop's exit, the bank president, Alexandre Martin, stepped in, took off his hat and addressed Odalie in English.

"Mademoiselle Markette. How nice to see you again. Meeting you in familiar places is becoming a habit. If I had my way, those chance meeting would increase."

"Why, Monsieur Martin, I had no idea that you could use the English language."

"Ah, Mademoiselle, in my business it is de rigueur. I fly to New York quite often, and by the way, I need a secretary to accompany me on such trips. Would you be interested?"

"Why, Monsieur Martin. While I would love to travel to the United States, I am afraid I would miss my little town of Blois. Does Madame Martin go to New York with you?"

"Ah, she is too busy to bother herself with business matters."

"What a shame to miss such an opportunity. On your next trip, I wish you a Bon voyage. Good day, Monsieur Martin."

Once again, Odalie Markette had sidestepped an unappreciated invitation. Her life had not yet been corrupted, and she was not yet ready for *une liaison dangereuse*. Since she was already out and about, Odalie decided to stop by Vern Sarvey's antique shop, and when she did, she got a surprise just looking in the display window. There, all polished up with some kind of preservative oil was the sign, and below it, in French, was a message which Odalie translated as:

> Could this be a long-lost sign board
> Taken by the poet, Francois Villon
> From some Parisian pub in the mid-
> 15th-century? Help me find out.
> Inquire within.

Attached to the base of Vernon's block of wood was the official French Department of Interior paper authenticating the age of the display piece in Vernon's shop window. The carbon dating designation could be read by any passerby. Odalie opened the antique shop door, the overhead bell sounded, and Vernon Sarvey showed his surprise and happiness by saying, "Mademoiselle Markette, what a pleasant surprise. What do you think of our discovery?"

"Monsieur Sarvey, I cannot take any credit for that find. But I do believe that your display will not only create interest, townspeople and tourists will soon be asking if they can touch that piece from the past."

"Odalie, I would never have imagined even thinking such a thing could be possible, but we have already had a dozen Blois citizens express their interest. One of the local bistro owners became so interested, he offered to purchase it immediately."

"What did you say?"

"I told him that I would inquire with my partner and added that she is a very discriminating young lady."

"Does she know that you sometimes over-embellish your responses to your customers' questions?"

"Could you return here later for dinner. I make a nice bouillabaisse, and the fish is fresh."

"Monsieur Sarvey, I would love that. We could talk about your next step with your new display item. It has potential."

"At 20:00 hours, everything will be ready. Can you join me?"

"By all means. I have a nice white wine which will enhance the meal."

The date was set. Odalie Markette was going to break her rules about associating with young men about town after dark. Those rules had already been stretched, but there was still room for enjoyment.

25

Vern Sarvey's kitchen, small, but well equipped, was located at the rear of his shop. It held a little table, four chairs, and it had been set with ceramic wear picked up along a road-side flea market in the area. Two wine glasses were arranged and waiting on Odalie's wine selection. Colorful napkins and cutlery which looked like real silver graced the table top. On a small gas stove, a pot of bouillabaisse boiled. The Mediterranean-style soup contained four different varieties of fish, one of which was local trout taken from the Loire. Vernon's bouillabaisse would compare favorably with that from any up-scale Parisian restaurant. Vernon was not leaving anything to chance this evening.

Odalie arrived minutes before the appointed time, and that pleased her host who kissed her on both cheeks and added a cozy hug at the end of the familiar greeting. As one would expect, Odalie, the guest in the home of a single, young man, offered her help in setting up or any other preparation that needed attention. Her host, Vernon, had made his best effort to have everything ready, and he took every opportunity to make sure his guest was comfortable being with him. And, that, being with Vernon, was still cause for concern.

Odalie had been on her own since she was a teenager. She did well at the university, but this was a new experience. She had become fond of her American lover. When the moment occurred for her to make a choice of giving herself to Vernon, she did not hesitate; she participated in their coupling actively and passionately, and that scared her. She was not accustomed to getting close to anyone in the past. She pondered over such things when Vern announced, "*A table!*"

Two candles provided just the right about of light for a romantic dinner. Vern has also set aside a colorful display of fresh flowers, a nice wine produced in the Loire Valley had been chosen, and Vern's specialty, bouillabaisse, allowed a wonderful aroma to fill the air and encourage the appetite. Polite conversation added to the perfect evening meal which acted as a catalyst for questions about Vern's family. Odalie was surprised to learn the Vernon's father was a well-known antique dealer in New Orleans, a city with a strong French history. When she asked why the son of an antique dealer would come to France and start a business, Vernon said, "My major at university was the French language and history. I believed that learning something about the trade here in France would lend itself to work back home. I had no idea that I would meet one of the most-beautiful young women in the country."

"Very interesting. I wonder who that person could be. Could it be Monique, my friend who owns the tea room next door? She is beautiful."

"Oh, no, this woman has already enhanced my business here. The more time I spend with her, the more important my business becomes. I want to see how far it goes."

"Your business or the association with this mysterious woman? Vern, before we talk anymore about the block of wood, where is this going between you and me?"

Before the antique dealer could answer, a loud crash was heard coming from the front of the shop. It sounded like a broken window, and for a brief moment, more glass was being shattered. Both Vernon and Odalie rose out of their seats, raced to the front of the store and saw two figures carrying off the sign board which had occupied the window in the front of the store. The two figures carrying the board placed it in a small truck-like van and rode off into the night. Vernon turned to Odalie and said, "Well the thing caught somebody's attention, didn't it."

26

Minutes after the verification of the broken store window, the missing 15th-century sign board, and the other collateral damage, cell phones were used to notify the local gendarme. Almost immediately, the familiar klaxon of European ambulances and patrol cars could be heard close by. As Vernon and Odalie inspected the victimized area, two French blue-colored patrol cars arrived on the scene. Showing no outward sign of concern, an officious-looking plain-clothed man showing no emotion or concern walked over to the Vernon's store front and inquired for the owner of the shop. Vern stepped up, introduced himself and began to explain what had happened. As soon as Odalie stepped closer to Vernon, the policeman's attention left the store owner, and he focused on Odalie. "Are you the store owner's wife, Madame?"

"No, Monsieur, I am a close friend."

The policeman once again addressed his questions to Vernon, wrote down some information on his official-looking pad, and continued with questions about the description of the items taken, a physical description of the perpetrators of the act, whether they had transportation, etc. Odalie once again caught the attention of the investigating officer, and she was asked the same questions. The entire question and answer session took almost a half hour. Identification cards were exchanged, and Vernon was asked to come into the local police office the very next day. No visible attempt was made to put out a search for the alleged thieves. Vernon was advised to close up his damaged window as best as possible, and the police went on their way. Both Vernon and Odalie hoped that a radio request had been made to track down both thieves and stolen item.

The sudden disappearance of anything, whether it be an inanimate thing once possessed or a loved one, brings instant remorse. If the thing lost was treasured, revered and was considered life-threatening, tears, despondency and the inability to function usually results. To Vernon Sarvey, a small business man in a foreign community, a destroyed shop window was not such a big thing. Yes, he was living on a budget, but the repair of his shop window would require a small bank loan. The item stolen had cost him a few euros, but that was not a big financial loss. The fact that the wooden sign board would not constitute a draw of interest from the public did bother him, and he expressed that fact to his friend, Odalie.

Odalie helped Vernon clean up the debris left behind in the robbery of the wooden block which was in the shop window. After a careful examination, nothing else had been touched. The excitement over the new antique item displayed must have reached a crescendo and reached the ears of someone who suspected that the publicity on the artifact might have been true. Odalie was alerted by Vern that he was going to speak to the bank president, Monsieur Martin the following morning and ask for a small loan to cover the cost of window repair. Odalie asked if he wanted her to accompany him to the bank, but Vern decided that he had already taken up too much of her time, and that he would contact her immediately after the meeting at the bank. That contact was made the very next evening by phone and Vernon said, "Odalie, you will never guess the result of my request for a loan. I had asked for ten-thousand euros which would have covered the cost of a new window and a few minor repairs to our front entrance. Monsieur Martin said that my business had not yet been established to garner a loan, and that I should wait until I had developed a more-substantial base of operations. What do you think of that?"

"Vernon, request another meeting for two days from now. I am going with you, but I do not want Monsieur Martin to know that I will be with you. Do you understand?"

"Yes. But…"

"Make the meeting, Vern. Call me when it is confirmed."

27

Two days later, Vernon called Odalie and told her that the meeting with the bank president was set for the following morning at 10 A.M. It was confirmed that Odalie would attend the meeting and that Monsieur Martin would not know that she would accompany Vernon to the meeting. Vern added, "Odalie, Monsieur Martin was not at all positive about changing his opinion about my loan." Odalie responded, "Vernon, men sometimes are put into a situation in which changing their minds all of a sudden seems to be the best for everyone. We shall see."

Vernon picked Odalie up on his way to the bank. She wore a low-cut, summer sundress. The dress was red with white polka dots, and it emphasized every curve, muscle and collateral benefits to the eye. Light but appropriate costume jewelry added another attraction to the entire outfit. Vernon wore his best suit, and he, looked like part of the bank staff when he walked in. Both Odalie and Vernon were offered seats, and they waited until called into Monsieur Martin's inner office.

The bank president's office was immaculately laid out. Oak-wood furnishings showed an expensive taste for a small-town banker. Monsieur Martin entered from his back room to his main office, and judging from facial expressions, he had not expected to see Odalie Markette. He immediately recovered and said, "Mademoiselle Markette, what a nice surprise. How nice to see you again. Are you now doing secretarial work for Monsieur Sarvey?"

"Not at all Monsieur Martin. But I love knowing more about-up-and coming entrepreneurs and banking. It gives me more to say when I attend outings or take tea with my friend, Monique."

"Ah, I understand. Now, Monsieur Sarvey. I thought we understood that a loan at this time would be unwise."

"Yes, Monsieur Martin. But business requires repetition of effort. I am sure that you understand."

Odalie interjected with, "Monsieur Martin, I wanted to respond to your offer of travel to the United States with you. Might I inquire with Madame Martin and gather her opinion?" Immediately, the bank president replied, "That won't be necessary. Madame will be out of town for several weeks visiting her parents in Paris. Perhaps we can see this thing through with Monsieur Sarvey after all. Monsieur Sarvey, the bank can lend you 10,000 euros, but the interest rate will be at seven percent." Odalie spoke up and said, "Monsieur Martin, things would go along much smoother if you were to consider how much a new shop in town would improve things for Blois. Let me suggest that you loan Monsieur Sarvey what his has requested and that the interest rate not be over two percent. That would allow me to perhaps help keep books for Monsieur Sarvey, and I would probably be too busy to inquire with Madame Martin about cross-ocean travel with her husband."

Minutes later, a contract was drawn up and signed giving Vernon Sarvey enough money to repair damage to his shop and then some. His interest rate was set at an unheard of low of one and one-half percent. Odalie and Vernon celebrated over a cup of tea with Odalie's friend Monique. The bank president fumed in his well-appointed office and knew that his transactions would never come to the attention of his wife…now in Paris.

28

Odalie, Vernon and their friend, Monique were into their second cup of tea when an official-looking police car pulled up to the front of the tea room. Two plane-clothes men got out and made their way to the front door of the store and walked into the tea room. One of the men, said, "Monsieur Sarvey?" to Vernon. Vernon's reply was quick and polite. The man addressing him continued, "Monsieur, we have located your table top. Two men, now in custody, told us that the former owner or the piece of wood that you and a beautiful young lady had deceived him saying that the sign or whatever it is was worth more than you paid. Do you have a receipt for the purchase of that piece of wood.?"

"Of course, officer. I happen to have it with me now."

Vernon retrieved the receipt which contained the description of the purchased item, price paid and date of purchase. He handed over his documents to the officer in front of him. The French officer read over the information, looked at Vernon and said, "Everything seems to be legitimate, Monsieur. You will be pleased to learn that two other men hired by Monsieur Paul Vauclud, the antique dealer, will be incarcerated along with the owner of the Meung-sur-Loire antique dealer. We have your wooden plank in our car. Will you take it now?"

"Yes, Sir, Officer. We will store it here until I get my car. Thank you for such a quick resolution of the problem, Sir."

Everyone shook hands, and the French policemen both lingered longer than necessary with both Odalie and Monique. Vernon thought, *I wonder if it's true what they say about French men.* A third cup of tea helped end a perfect day for everyone but the antique dealer from Meung-sur-Loire and his two hired thugs. When the policemen returned the sign board to Monique's shop, Vernon excused himself and returned to his shop to get his automobile. Monique turned to Odalie and said, "Let me guess how you two will celebrate the return of your stolen item. If we could film that celebration, Odalie, you would be a star of screen and stage."

"Monique, you are not funny. And, if the celebration does take place, I will keep the details to myself."

"Ah, my good friend. That will give me all the more reason to embellish my pent-up emotions to my customers."

"Monique, you wouldn't...would you?"

"Certainly not. However, I expect some interesting feedback when we next have tea."

"Monique, I love you, but you are terrible."

29

Vernon immediately asked Odalie to help him decide where to display his retrieved relic. She, in her desire to continue her relationship with the young American, assured him that she would happily collaborate with him on that subject. They both agreed that such a piece should not be displayed in the store's front window. While it would draw the public's interest, it would also invite a smash-and-grab circle of thieves. Instead, the 15 th-century-artifact would take a prominent place in the middle of the store, and its provenance boldly printed out for all to see. In the following days, there was a constant flow of citizens, tourists and people shopping for something unique. But the wooden board was the drawing card, and Vernon often heard from viewers of the piece, "Do think it possible...that Villon might have touched it?"

Business in the newest shop in town was booming, and the young American entrepreneur was proud of his enterprise. He also knew that a certain beautiful young lady had played an important role in the success of his endeavor.

Odalie Markette had once again helped someone achieve their dreams. In the past, after that success had taken place, she usually moved on and would seek out someone in need of direction. However, Vernon Sarvey was different. He showed himself to be good, trusting and forgiving. He did not press charges against Monsieur Vauclud, the former owner of his prized possession. Instead, he left that to the authorities. The French safety department knew how far to pursue such things. What Odalie did, however, was in conflict with her past *modus operandi*. She had benefitted economically from helping others, but she was not ready to move on. She might have fallen in love.

One afternoon, a well-dressed man in his late sixties stopped in front of Vernon's antique shop and took in very carefully items on display. The suit he wore resembled what some banker, attorney or prominent person might wear. Shined shoes, an appropriate colored tie to go with his outer wear and an air of authority about his posture. The man pushed open the front door, put the little bell at the entrance in action and proceeded to look over other articles on display. His entry drew the attention of Vernon, but instead of immediately addressing a person who might be just browsing, the shop owner expertly stood aside and waited until a request for information, price or clarification was called for. But the thing which held the new customer's attention was the 15th-century-artifact.

Without touching the wooden sign board, the interesting individual read every information card relating to the sign. Placed his hand to his chin and pondered the piece as if he were conducting some kind of criminal investigation or observing the antics of a person showing loss of memory or body function. Finally, he called for Vernon's attention and asked, "Excuse me, Monsieur, are you the proprietor of this shop?" Vernon politely answered, "Yes, Sir, my name is Vernon Sarvey, and I am the owner of this store." The mysterious man replied, "My name is Monsieur Rene Toussaint, the Director of the *Bibliotheque Nationale* in Paris, and I am here on official business on behalf of the French Republic." Sarvey responded, "Very impressive, Sir. What brings you to the village of Blois?"

"Well, Monsieur, it has been reported that you claim to have a piece of history related to the poet, Francois Villon. Such a claim, Monsieur, could be misconstrued and could border on being an attempt at fraud."

"That is understood. However, at no time was it ever stated or printed that this piece had ever touched the hands of the poet. That it is from the same time period of the poet's life has been authenticated via carbon dating. The testing was done here in Blois at the official Bureau of Measures."

"If that is the case, Monsieur Sarvey, that item, the block of wood, might be sold and purchased by any passerby."

"That, Monsieur Toussaint, is partly true. However, I have no intention of selling the relic."

"The *Bibliotheque* has authorized me to offer you one-hundred euros for your block of wood."

"As stated previously, Monsieur, that particular items is not for sale. It is offered as a relic from the past and a reminder of what could have been."

"I could offer as much as two-hundred euros, but that is all."

"I am sorry, Monsieur Toussaint. The artifact will remain as one of my most-sought after articles and remain the center piece of the establishment."

"If that is your final decision, Monsieur Sarvey, I must warn you that the French Government covets its past, and if necessary, might legally step in and confiscate that item without any outlay of funds."

"What a wonderful way to publicize my small business. I would pay nothing for months of free advertising. Let's ponder that."

Nothing more was said, and the Director of the *Bibliotheque Nationale* stroud out into the street and went on his way. Upon Odalie's advice, articles in the local news reported that an official from a government office had offered to purchase *Le Pot du Diable* sign board at an undisclosed cost. Interest in and traffic to and from Vernon's now-thriving antique shop grew disproportionately to the size of the 3' x 4' wooden block. Vernon and Odalie celebrated that evening, and no one complained about the on and off vocal expressions of pleasure emanating from the open upstairs window of Odalie's cottage.

30

It was hard to believe that a single item hanging in a place of business, not having any direct official authentication of origin, could influence interest, increase obsessive buying of trinkets located close to the source of that addiction, and start a parade about something located in an antique shop. But Vernon's block of wood, his supposed sign board dating from the 15th-century, did just that. The citizens of Blois felt as if they had something equal to one of Napoleon's many Arcs of Triumphs located throughout France. The artifact in Vernon Sarvey's sign board soon became known as, 'Villon's Business Card'. And that just increased the mystique surrounding what Sarvey had in his possession of things from the past.

Odalie Markette, single, voluptuous, small-town beauty from Blois, had a dilemma. While she was enjoying her very close relationship with her young American entrepreneur, she was unsure as to where her association with him was going. She enjoyed the freedom of coming and going as she pleased. She had done well seeing to others and helping them realize their dreams, but she had dreams, too. Every capable, socially and gifted young woman does. Vernon Sarvey had all the redeeming qualities that any young woman might desire. His conduct with others was not only appropriate, he had drawn the attention of the residents of Blois as being well-mannered, proud of his position in the community, and, if Odalie were more-observant, other young, single and readily available women in town were ready to step up, be escorted and reward him with their favors.

Sarvey's little antique shop already had the reputation of being important to the health of the community. Tourists were drawn to his shop, and they lingered a day or two more in the city because of their need to browse over things they did not recognize. His shop was becoming well known to tour-bus drivers, and stopping at Vernon's store soon became a highlight of things to see and do. But to Odalie, she still pondered what Vernon's intentions were toward her. Vernon had not made any direct overtures of making their relationship more socially firm. He seemed to be playing the field and not in any solid way making things more permanent. While their intimacy had been passionate and physically pleasing, it was hard to put a definite direction on where things might be headed.

Vernon Sarvey had grown up in New Orleans. He was used to the comings and goings of vacationing thrill seekers and strangers who lingered no more that a week or two in his city. Vernon had attended and earned a degree in geological science from Tulane University, and he had become adept at looking at a piece of rock and determining its age and whether it might be a good idea to dig, mine or prospect for valuable minerals, gas or oil. He had also become proficient in recognizing the value of semi-precious stones and the ancient remains of animals which had inhabited the earth millions of years ago. Such knowledge had led to his adding such things to his collection of things past to his shop in Blois.

While attending college in his home town, he had worked at his father's downtown antique shop, and he was schooled on what it took to run a thriving business. Vernon's father had intended his son to take over his shop when he retired. Vernon had not put that idea aside, but he wanted to learn more about the trade and decided to do so on his own in a country known for respecting things from the past. He wanted to know if he had the desire and experience to do well on his own. So, the little town in Blois is where he found himself. It is also where he was falling in love with a young French woman, and he, too, shared a dilemma. What might be his next steps with this woman whose beauty and verve had so fascinated him?

31

More than several days had gone by before Vernon reached out to Odalie by phone. After repeated rings with no one answering, Vernon left a message, "Odalie, the last few days have been very busy at my shop. We are at the peak of the tourist season, and many people have visited the store. As you might expect, our wooden sign board drew the most interest. I have had more offers from those who wanted to buy it than ever before. One American bar owner from New York City wanted to display it behind his trendy bar on Wall Street. I did not accept the offer which was considerable. Odalie, I need your opinion on something. Please call me back."

Odalie listened to Vernon's message, but she did not answer immediately. A fisherman's line in the water often is neglected by the hungriest of fish. Odalie's appetite for social and sexual excitement had increased, but the taste of such things is sometimes more satisfying by waiting for the proper moment.

The wooden sign board once again drew interest. Someone from some official office in Paris, perhaps Rene Toussaint from the *Bibliotheque Nationale,* had informed journalists at Paris Match, the social/political tabloid so popular throughout the world, that an ancient relic, one perhaps connected to one of France's most-famous poets, was on display in a little antique shop in the city of Blois. When that story broke in a picture-less article, train tickets from Paris to Blois were selling like reduced-cost French pastries. Thrill seekers, tourists and prospective antique speculators flocked to Vernon's store, and he needed help in running his business. The first person Vernon thought of was Odalie Markette, not only as a possible employee, but perhaps something more. Vernon gave her a call.

"Why, Vernon. Good to hear from you. How are you?"

"Odalie, first off, let me say that I miss you, and let me tell you why.

Odalie, in the past, there never seemed to be time or the desire to be with someone, someone like you, a beautiful woman, intelligent, the spirit to enjoy life. I am finding that I need that certain something in my life. Your presence when I am with you lifts me up like no other person. Let me express more to you face to face."

For a very short time, the silence over the electronic freeway disturbed Vernon. He said nothing. He was patient. Finally, Odalie spoke saying, "Vernon, those words are beautiful. I do have feeling for you. Our nights together should reinforce that for you. There is still much I want to do in this life. We should talk about this. I am meeting Monique at her tea shop tomorrow at noon. Could you drop in an hour after that?"

"I will be there. Thank you, Odalie. See you tomorrow."

32

The next day, Odalie kept her appointment with the tearoom-owner, Monique. Among the things they discussed was how the tourist business was going in the city, what Monique's love life was like, and, of course, how Odalie was handling her close friend, Vernon Sarvey. Their meeting finished early, and Monique returned to her booth behind a counter just a few steps away while Odalie finished her tea. She had no idea of what was about to happen. There were no preemptive signs of what was coming. But in walked Alexandre Martin, the bank president. Without asking, he took a chair at Odalie's table and said, "Mademoiselle Markette, you could awake the sexual desire of Napoleon Bonaparte. I would like to personally witness such a thing. What would it cost me?"

Monique, standing nearby but within hearing range could not believe the audacious and discourteous language she heard coming from the bank president's mouth. During her get togethers with her friend, Odalie, she had learned enough English to recognize right from wrong, but she gave no indication of her understanding of the proposition just voiced by the man sitting at Odalie's table, but she did know that her friend was about to react, so she waited.

Odalie took her time, tasted her tea and looked up at the man sitting close to her. Then, looking the bank president eye-to-eye, she said, "Monsieur Martin, I am going to overlook your rude and shameless use of the English language. I am going to wipe the excrement from my mind you just deposited, and I am going to go on with my life in this wonderful little city by the Loire. I will, however, retain my opinion of you, but it is not worth stating at the moment."

Martin remained calm and responded with, "Odalie, I know that you have been keeping company with the American antique dealer, and it is no secret that you have been giving yourself freely to him and many occasions; your evening verbal expressions of pleasure have been reported to me by your neighbors, and people talk. Having someone nearby to share in your desires of the flesh is not a crime. What will it take. I am well off, and my wife has her own dallying with male acquaintances of her choosing." Odalie looked at Martin with some disdain and said, "Aren't you afraid someone will hear these confessions?" "Odalie, he said, there is no one here who can speak or understand English, no priest present, and your friend, Monique, is too dense to be able to understand English let alone French."

Monique made no gesture of having understood what was just uttered. She busied herself with wiping down counters and doing what a shop keeper does when customers are talking. But Odalie did respond by getting up from her table, paying her bill and saying goodbye to her friend, Monique. She said nothing to the cur of a man still sitting at her table. As if he were some casualty on some now-silent battlefield, the bank president remained silent.

33

It is difficult trying to understand the perversion of some men and women. Is it some mysterious urge that leads them to believe that self-gratification is worth the effort and that no crime has been committed if an acquaintance is a willing participant? Whatever the case, Alexandre Martin, President of one of Blois' biggest banks, had just propositioned a young resident of his city, and from all the evidence, he thought himself innocent of any wrong doing. As he left the tea shop, he made no attempt to acknowledge its owner, Monique Mayes. She, too, in her contempt for the man leaving her shop, made the man invisible in her mind. She did, however, think back to what she had heard the bank president say to her friend, Odalie. Monique's English was good enough to lead her to believe that the man leaving her establishment was a scoundrel.

What does the woman do when she has been verbally insulted and invited to take part in a devious endeavor? If you are Odalie Markette, you walk away proudly, consider the sources of your displeasure, and continue on with your life. But Odalie would keep what had just happened in her memory bank, and if and when appropriate, she would recall that information stored like some weapon for use in an emergency. Odalie continued on her way toward home, but she had some marketing to do. She stopped at her out-door market, and looked over items that she might need. She had invited her friend, Vernon, for a late-night dinner during the week, and she wanted that dinner to be special. The fish stand caught her eye, and some fresh perch recently caught in the nearby river looked good. Odalie was familiar with all the merchants in the market, and the fishmonger quickly said his greetings to one of his best customers. He admired Odalie because he knew about her ability to help others. In is native language he said, "Good morning, Mademoiselle Markette. How are you this morning?" Odalie responded with, "Good morning, Monsieur. Your perch looks like it is fresh from the river. Would you recommend it today.?" The Frenchman responded, "Yes, it is among our most asked-for fish, and it comes from this region."

Odalie purchased a pound and a half of the good-looking fish, and as she was about to continue on her way, the fish merchant said, "Miss Markette, Monsieur Martin passed by just a short while ago, and I overheard him speaking to the market manager. He was saying bad things about you. Be careful". Odalie thanked her friend, the fish seller and continued on her way. But she did wonder what kind of nastiness was now going on with the bank president. She went directly home and called Vernon and invited him to dinner saying, "Vernon, I need some advice. When you come to dinner this evening, I will clarify all that." Vernon acknowledged the invitation. He loved fresh fish, but he was more attracted to the person who was going to prepare it. Vernon Sarvey was falling in love with Odalie Markette.

34

Around 7 P.M. that evening, Vernon arrived at Odalie's door and politely knocked before entering. He had not pushed his luck on assuming that he had all the privileges that sometimes go with male and female relationships. That Odalie was a willing participant in their love making, and that she had coached him in the French way of a man making love to a woman, it in no way opened the door to every and all opportunities usually restricted to married couples. And, as to Vernon's enjoying his relationship with this fascinating woman, never once did she ever turn away from his suggestion that she put her legs in the air for him. He considered himself lucky in every way possible, and before the night was out, his luck would improve in spades with Odalie; she was an equal-opportunity advocate.

Later that evening after the love making, Odalie turned to her partner and said, "Vern, my friend, Monique brought something to my attention today. It has to do with the run-down chateau just miles from here."

"OK, what did she say?"

"The chateau has been abandoned for years, and its furniture will soon be up for auction. Are we interested?"

"Your use of the word, 'we' is music to my ears. I like the sound of that. What might they have for sale?"

"The furniture is not Louis V, but the mirror in the ballroom probably has seen French Royalty from Louis XIV to Napoleon Bonaparte pass in front of it. And, there is a rumor about the mirror you know."

"No, I am afraid gossip has eluded me on that subject so far in my stay here in *la belle France,* but something tells me that you, my beautiful lady, are going to fill me in."

"Well, you, Vern, have already filled me. Quite adequately I must say. Let me return the favor by telling you what people say about the chateau's mirror."

"I am at your disposal my lady. What have you heard about this mysterious mirror from the past?"

35

For the next half hour and while her body wore no night clothing other than a light bed spread, Odalie offered up a short overview of the history of the Chateau de Blois. Vernon, her lover, he, too, without a stitch of anything covering his body and sharing only the light bed covering with the woman beside him, listened patiently. He had studied French history, and the Loire Valley, and its history intrigued him. But the entry portion of Odalie's summary of the chateau was not as captivating as was her body's attributes. That was understood. After all, Vernon was in love with this woman who had stolen his heart, mind and body.

Odalie continued her story about the town's most impressive building by saying that the castle's history dated back to the fourteenth century and that Joan of Arc, in her military campaign against the English, had been blessed by the Archbishop of Reims before the battle of Orleans in 1429. She recounted that Francois I, the benefactor of Leonardo de Vinci, had installed the Italian artist in the chateau for a short time, and that the painter of the Mona Lisa was interred on the chateau's grounds. In the 15 hundreds, a thousand Protestants were murdered and hung out the windows of the chateau and their bodies later flung into the Loire River running by. Charles d'Orleans, the French poet, had taken up residence in the chateau after having spent twenty-five years as an English prisoner in the Tower of London. Odalie added that Charles, a promoter of poetry, had also befriended the greatest French poet, Francois Villon, and that he, too, had visited the chateau. But it was not all the prominent and historic personalities that held Odalie's interest. It was the mirror, that 8' by 10' piece of treated glass, that once was hung in the great meeting hall of the Chateau de Blois. A mirror that had probably captured the reflection of all the people just mentioned.

Odalie, still lying warm and close to Vernon, was suddenly made aware that her lover had become sexually aroused once again. But she still had much to say before she would give herself to the man lying beside her. Odalie very subtly changed her position and told Vern that she had more to say. She began by saying, "Vern, as I mentioned previously, it has been rumored that some people, those who have attended antique sales and auctions at which the chateau's mirror was on display, that on occasion, the attendees at such functions swore that they caught glimpses of characters in period clothing floating on the surface of that ancient glass."

"Yes, Odalie, but you do know that people in closed places like a museum or sales room sometimes get caught up in the moment when on vacation or squeezed in a small area. Some of my friends told me that one of the high-school age American tourists swore that she saw Catherine de Medici at the top of the stairs in Chenonceaux castle. And, my father once told me that one of his customers in his New Orleans antique shop was certain that she caught sight of Andrew Jackson in one of the shop's looking glasses."

"I am sure that there is some truth to all that. Let me ask you this: could we go to the auction tomorrow and see the mirror in question. If I see one of my heroines, I assure you that I will keep my sighting to myself."

"OK, but I do not want to see you spirited away into some ancient piece of glass. I am addicted to you and your worldly presence."

A passionate kiss was his immediate reward. That kiss would lead to many others.

36

The Auction House, a well-known business in the city of Blois, was located in a far corner of the Chambord Train Station. The depot, a building of steel and glass patterned after things constructed at the beginning of the twentieth century, blended in well with the older part of the town. The rail hub served as a jumping off place for the south of France, and the trains coming in and going out of this popular destination spot were the modern electric-powered bullet trains. They were fast, comfortable and quiet unlike the diesel-powered work horses of mass haulers in other countries.

At the Auction House, a crowd had already formed inside its enclosure, and its occupants were dressed as if going to the races at Dauville. Flowery dresses, three-piece suits and polished footwear hinted at a seriousness not usually seen in this tourist area of the country. Old things had attracted a lot of interested people. Others in the crowd, history buffs, onlookers and some legitimate antique dealers made for an interesting mix. On tables, collectables such a bowls, flatware, lamps and other parlor furniture were appropriately positioned. No prices were attached to any of the items on display. But it was the mirror, that piece of the past which probably captured the images of French history, off to one corner of things to be auctioned, which drew the most interest. And like most auctioneers, the mirror would be the last item brought before the public.

Once the auction began, things started to fly off the display tables and disappear outside to waiting transport vehicles. The money spent on these first-offered items left little to be wagered on the house's most prize item, the mirror. And, waiting his turn to place a bid on that item was none other than the bank president, and Odalie's nemesis, Alexandre Martin. Martin was in the middle of a crowd of well-dressed auction goers who were fitted out with stylish suits, gowns and colorful hats. But even with his entourage, Martin's eyes were focused in the voluptuous Odalie Markette.

Odalie wore a strapless light-colored summer dress. She was not bogged down by pretentiousness of dress, and she had nothing to prove. Besides, she was escorted by the young American antique dealer who was getting rave attention from a Villon-related piece of history which stood just inside his little shop. Odalie and her escort drew admiring glances from both men and women. It did not take long for the bank president, Martin, to officially greet the couple to the day's event.

Monsieur Martin, in spite of being in the company of his wife and her friends, bolted from his group and darted toward where Odalie had taken up her observation area of the soon-to-take place auction. Like a dirt-bike rider on some small city street, Martin sped toward his target and without addressing Odalie's escort, the young antique dealer from America, Martin said, "Mademoiselle Markette, you and your radiant summer dress lend dignity and beauty to today's auction."

"Monsieur Martin, what are your interests here in this sale of old and valuable things?"

"Why, Mademoiselle, as you have been told before, you, the most beautiful woman in Blois, are the star attraction in today's display of desired things."

Odalie did not in any way acknowledge the bank president's compliments. Instead, she took time to introduce her escort. "Please say Hello to the up and coming antique dealer in all of France, Mr. Vernon Sarvey" Alexandre Martin, a man used to shunning anyone not affiliated with banking, nodded in Sarvey's direction but did not offer his hand as a friendly gesture. Vernon made no effort extend his hand either. Instead, he excused himself telling Odalie that he needed a closer look at some of the items to be auctioned before the sale began. The bank president used Vernon's departure to move closer to the most beautiful woman at the day's event, and he said to her, "Mademoiselle Markette, what brings you to today's outing?"

"Oh, I never question Mr. Sarvey's reasons for looking at beautiful things. He's quite good at everything he does. We are very good friends."

"And, how has he found you, Odalie? A good discovery or a bad discovery?"

"Well, Monsieur Martin, something tells me that Mr. Sarvey comes away from me being very, how should we say, 'very satisfied'"

"I wonder if I could be tested by you one of these days, Mademoiselle."

"You might want to ask your wife, Madame Martin, she is looking this way and is beaconing to you as we speak."

The bank president returned to his wife's clutch faster than a penned-up rooster. The auction was about to begin.

37

Auctions demand well-defined functions. Organizers, sellers, buyers and assistants, including trained auctioneers are informed about an impending sale of collected items from various locations and historic areas. Most items for sale carry a provenance, a distinct place of origin or source. Such pieces carry with them a history of having played a part in the growth of an area, town or country, and if authenticated, such collections demand prices which can make a buyer or seller a small fortune. The auction house at Blois was known for offering items which once played important roles in the lives of famous French people and their homes or castles. At any auction, one of the first things which takes place is the preview period, a spot and time when items for sale are examined, researched and scrutinized. Appraisals are discussed among visitors, sellers and buyers, estate executors and crowds at such a preview period often predict a starting price for pieces on display.

A large crowd at an auction does point to higher prices for things up for sale. When an object is sold, an appraisal commission for both seller and buyer is charged. That lowers the auction fee collected by the house, and that fee is sometimes 50% of the item's final price. Buyers are given paddles if they are considered legitimate, and the buyer raises or waves his paddle to the auctioneer once the bidding begins. All bidding ends when the auctioneer hammers his gavel and calls out, "Sold". Today's auction was about to begin.

Odalie, sitting close to Vernon and making no attempt to hide her feelings for the American from others, especially the bank president, watched the proceedings attentively. The fabled mirror was brought into view, and its surface shimmered in the sunlight seeping through the glass in the overhead ceiling. A slight rumble could be heard among the attendees, and the auction on the antique piece of furniture and decoration began. All of a sudden, Vernon handed Odalie his auction paddle, and without a word being said, she waved her paddle, and the auctioneer stated, "Opening bid from the lady at the side of the room, starts at 1,500 euros. The leading contender for the purchase of the mirror, Alexandre Martin, looked surprised; he had thought that he would be bidding against Odalie's supposed lover, but he waved his paddle and the price for the mirror went up to 2,000 euros. Paddles waved, the crowd 'Oo'd' and 'Ah'ed' and the price rose to 3,000 euros. Martin waved his paddle three times, and that drove the price to 6,000 euros. Odalie did nothing. Just as the auctioneer was about to hammer the auction of the mirror closed, Martin began congratulating himself by talking to his entourage. Odalie waved her paddle, the auctioneer waited the required seconds and then hammered his gavel and yelled, "Sold to the young woman in the beautiful dress." The final price for the mirror, a period piece from the sixteenth century, was 6,500 euros. The steal of the day.

38

As expected, auction goers, bidders and friends, especially Monique, the tea-room owner, mobbed Odalie and congratulated her on her purchase. The bank president and his wife had disappeared as soon as the word, 'sold' was sounded out. No one asked her where she had gotten the money for the mirror's purchase, but her benefactor, Vernon, stood close by and marveled at the attention his very close friend was getting. Nothing was said about Vernon's father, the antique dealer from New Orleans who provide the funds needed for his son to start a business in France. That information was shared only with Odalie, the young beautiful woman about town who had captured the young American's heart and mind. Later that evening, both young lovers would celebrate in another sharing---their bodies. That exchange would take hours, and conversations about what to do with the mirror took place as respites between lovemaking sessions. Champagne corks popped and so did a lot of other things.

Three days later, the fabled mirror was delivered to Vernon's antique shop, and it was placed alongside a beer-hall sign dating from the fifteenth century. They seemed to fit and blend together in the twenty-first century, and while it seemed strange to Vernon, the two pieces, dating from perhaps the same century, time and place, looked as though they belonged together. There was a renewed interest in the two pieces, and tourists began to show more enthusiasm as they looked upon the two oldsters, the mirror and the beer-hall sign. Business was good for the American entrepreneur.

In the days following the acquisition of the historic mirror, Vernon's little antique business seemed to glow with new life. His shop became the talk of the city. Everyone wanted to see the fabled piece of glass which had reflected the images of past heroes and their queens. The mirror's popularity inspired buyers of lesser things such as the copper bathtub of Marie Antoinette, a wash basin which supposedly wetted the fingers of Louis XIV at Versailles, and bayonets used by soldiers who fought with and against Napoleon I. Vernon Sarvey, American expatriate, was having the time of his life; he seemed to have won the heart of the most beautiful woman in town, and he was accumulating a small fortune for his efforts.

Odalie shared her young lover's enthusiasm and interest in this latest purchase, the looking glass. She had just received Vernon's invitation for an evening viewing of his newest acquisition, and she volunteered to host the event with him. The showing of the mirror alongside a beer-hall sign which might have inspired the pen of France's greatest poet, Francois Villon. The Friday-night viewing of the above antiques was to take place at 7 P.M., and attendees arrived early in clothing worn mostly for Friday-night mass. Perhaps they thought that one of history's most fascinating persons would suddenly materialize out of the mirror and chide them for inappropriate dress.

Chairs were placed in a semi-circle and offered all the viewers a clear shot at taking in the mirror's reflection. To add to the mystique, lights were angled on the entire surface of the antique mirror. The mirror seemed to glow of its own accord and seemed to beacon to onlookers to venture closer and see themselves in the same glass that might have held ancient portraits of passers-by. Some of those who captured themselves in the mirror would smile and then wave goodbye to themselves or to an imaginary partner from the past. All was well until…from the back of the seated viewers, a young girl blurted out, "Maman, il y a quelqu'un dans le miroir. C'est un homme, et il porte un costume." Among those startled by the child's outburst were Odalie and Vernon who, at first amused, then disturbed; they had not counted on an apparition taking place. The child's mother tried to calm her daughter saying, "Tais-toi. Ce sont les son et lumieres". Vernon knew quite well that he had not hired a light and sound system, the usual source of added excitement at night showings.

To the dismay of the evening's host, the young American antique dealer, several of the mirror viewers started to leave the event. As they approached the shop's door, some of them said, "Well, Sir, you do put on a great show. We'll be back for more." Odalie just shook her head in disbelief as did her lover, Vernon. Both the organizers of the evening wished attendees well as they left the shop. Once the visitors to the event had all departed, Odalie turned to Vernon and said, "Mon amour, I need a *coup de rouge*. Will you join me?" Vernon did not hesitate in answering, "*Cela va sans dire*. I like red wine, and I love the person who suggested it."

39

Later that same evening, after both Odalie and Vernon had quenched their thirst for each other, they lay side by side and out of breath. Vernon turned toward his lover and said, "Odalie, what did that little girl see tonight?"

"Vern, we must first respect the fact that she is a child. Children often get emotional during big gatherings. They get caught up in the moment of excitement. And, don't forget, that little girl, along with others, had listened to your pre-viewing explanation of who among historic characters might have seen themselves in that mirror."

"That's true. But the child did say specifically that she saw a man dressed in some kind of costume. And, that might have meant clothing worn by 15th or 16th century inhabitants."

Not much more was discussed about the little girl's sighting. Both Odalie and her lover were spent in their coupling from a strong sexual attraction. Vernon wondered why the town's most beautiful woman had been giving herself to him. He was neither wealthy nor destitute. Yes, he was handsome and handled himself well with others. He wondered what might be the next steps in this relationship he had come to treasure. Sleep and dreams robbed him of further thought in this matter.

The next day, both the antique dealer and his love interest went their separate ways. Vern busied himself with administrative and planning chores in his shop. He made sure that the mirror and related time-period items were arranged where the public could see them from street level. Odalie decided to visit her friend, Monique, the tea room owner. She had seen her friend at last evening's reception, and Odalie was interested in knowing what Monique thought about the event. As soon as Odalie stepped into Monique's tea room, the owner rushed up to her and said, "Odalie, before you even sit down, I have something to tell you about last night. You must listen to me…that little girl's statement about seeing something in the mirror…I saw it, too. Come to a table. I'll join you, and I will tell you what I saw."

Monique organized her employees. Then, she and Odalie sat down at a table a short distance from the entrance to the tea room. Once seated, Monique began by saying, "Odalie, I am Catholic and so is my family. We don't believe in illusions, figments of the imagination or sorcery. But I do believe that there are things in our world that cannot be explained using simple logic."

"Monique, as long as I have known you, I would never doubt anything you had to say. I trust you, and other than Vern, you are my closest friend."

"Thank you, Odalie. Now, just listen to me. Last night at the showing of the mirror and other items in Vern's shop, I was standing directly behind the little girl who was looking at the mirror. I, too, was focused on the thing. All of a sudden, the surface of the mirror became hazy. At first, I thought that someone in a haste to clean the surface of the mirror might have left a smudge. Looking closer, behind that smoky surface, a figure emerged…the image of a man. Odalie, at the university, I was a student of French history, and I studied drawings and paintings of historical personalities. Odalie, the man portrayed in the mirror was wearing clothing worn in the 15th and 16th centuries. Not only that, the figure in the mirror had a writing instrument in his hand, a quill, and he was writing something on a hand-held board. When the little girl interrupted the audience and told us what she saw, the image in the mirror slowly dissolved as if he was a madeleine in a cup of tea."

"Monique, I don't quite know what to say. Did you have champaign before the showing?"

"Odalie, that is not funny. And, yes, like the others, I did sample Vern's liquid refreshments. But the little girl didn't, and she saw what I saw."

"Monique, have you told anyone else about this?"

"No, not even Jean-Claude, my boyfriend."

"This evening, Vern is stopping by my home around 7 P.M. Could you join us for a glass of wine and tell him your story?"

"I'll be there promptly. And, I might pass on the wine. Maybe not.

40

That same day at 7 P.M., Monique arrived at Odalie's home, knocked at her door and was greeted by Vernon Sarvey who had arrived earlier. Vernon greeted Monique warmly. He liked Odalie's friend primarily because Vernon liked anything and anyone connected to the woman to whom he had become attached romantically and often physically. Vern conducted Monique into the parlor, offered her a glass of Bordeaux rouge, and Monique accepted the wine with a thank you. Odalie joined them almost immediately, and all three began talking at once. The topic of conversation was the strange sighting which took place at Vernon's reception at his antique shop last evening.

After a little coaxing, Monique recounted her story about what she had witnessed just twenty-four hours previously. A word-for-word rendition of what she had told Odalie was given to Vernon. At the end of Monique's verbal account, Vernon said, "Ladies, what are we going to do with what we just heard? Do we drop it as if it had not taken place? Or, do we investigate this thing further?" Odalie answered, "How would we go about doing an investigation of something which might never occur again?" Vernon replied, "You know, it is not only Monique's disclosure of what she saw. We have a little girl who stated the same thing." Monique said, "Vernon, do you know who the little girl was? Her mother comes into my tea room almost every day, and the girl's father is the mayor of Blois."

Monique continued by saying, "The mayor's name is Clement LeCours. His wife, Janine, is a sweetheart, and she sometimes brings her daughter into my tea parlor after school. The daughter's name is Paulette, and she, too, is nice and well mannered. Should I inquire with the mother whether we could talk to the daughter?" Vernon answered, "That might be very touchy. The girl's father is a politician, and he is respected by everyone in the city." Odalie added, "You know, we could spread the word that we are looking for anyone who attended the showing of the mirror and ask whether anything strange occurred that evening." Monique responded, "Odalie, that sounds like a good idea. If anyone comes forward, it would be of their own free will, and we, then, would not be accused of spreading a rumor of an out-of-this-world sighting."

In less that two-day's time, Odalie's church affiliation helped her put in a request to anyone who attended Vern's antique-shop viewing of the mirror and related items and who might have witnessed anything strange to contact her or the antique dealer. Monique, Odalie's friend and tea-room owner, posted a similar request in her shop for all to see. A short time later, both venues delivered feedback on the requests for information. The parish priest at Odalie's church reported that several of his parishioners claimed that there was a certain uneasiness in Vern's shop that evening. The priest added that the price of items on display might have been cause for that uneasiness. Monique said that something similar had been noted, but no specifics about strange sights were unfolded. Monique did say that Madame LeCours, the mayor's wife, told her that the mayor's daughter, Paulette, was willing to speak to the antique dealer and that the mayor and his wife were in agreement with their daughter's willingness to speak. Vernon sat up a meeting between the mayor, his family and others such as Odalie, Vern himself and Monique. That meeting was to take place on Friday at the end of the week.

The meeting with the already-named parties took place in Vern's antique parlor promptly at 7 P.M. All parties were present. A very cordial atmosphere resulted, and the mayor himself was amused that his daughter had perhaps witnessed a phenomenon common with young children, and he attributed his daughter's sighting to the excitement of the moment. While the adults discussed such a bizarre happening, Paulette, the mayor's daughter, wandered around the antique shop taking in the display of things old and salvaged. A short while later, the adults heard what sounded like a conversation going on in the area of the mirror a short distance away. Madame LeCours got up to investigate because she recognized her daughter's voice. When she arrived at her daughter's side, she noticed that Paulette's eyes were fixed on the glass in the mirror. The mother said, "Paulette, were you talking to someone just now?" Paulette replied, "Maman, I was asking the man in the mirror to talk to me again. But I think that he is too shy."

Both the mother and her daughter rejoined the adults in Vern's shop, and Madame LeCours said, "Monsieur le Maire, we must go. These kind people need to rest." Then, the mayor's wife turned to Vernon, shook his hand and said, "Mr. Sarvey, you might have an unwanted guest in your antique shop. But he could make you famous, and the city, too." Vernon's entourage, the few that they were, looked at each other with amazement and wonder. No one said a word.

41

Later that evening, lying close together in Odalie's bed, Vernon snuggled close and allowed his hands to slowly trace the voluptuous body of the woman to whom he just made love, and whispered in her ear, "Odalie, do you think that there is another man in our lives?"

"Vern, you are the only man I want in my life. But in your antique parlor, that is another question. As long as he stays under glass, we will be fine."

"We will discuss that. But right now, the man lying close to you would like to explore you one more time before we sleep."

"Well, Mr. Darwin, have at it."

And he did. New and wonderful places were visited and enjoyed.

During the next few days, the city of Blois returned to normal. Tourists flooded the streets and shops, townspeople did their thing and the weather was such that everyone enjoyed themselves doing what pleased them. The mayor and his wife kept a close watch on their daughter, Paulette. Monique entertained visitors to her tea room, and the most-talked about thing in town was the idea that a simple antique mirror might have captured history in its reflection.

Vernon Sarvey was profiting from such rumors, and sales of items from his antique shop soared. Odalie Markette, for the first time in her life, was falling in love with an American entrepreneur, and she liked it. She was fascinated with a man who had brought mystery and physical excitement into her life, and she wanted more. Odalie did wonder how far this feeling might lead, and she did realize that what brought her close to Vernon was a magnetism which could not be denied.

Days later, Vern placed a call to Odalie and said, "Hey, Odalie, here's something interesting. Moments ago, a man from some museum in Paris stopped by the shop and offered us fifty-thousand euros for our mirror."

"Our mirror, Vern?"

"Yes, of course, our mirror. I want you with me on this…and other things, too."

"That makes me happy, Vern. What are we going to do?"

"Let's talk about it. Are you busy tonight around 8? And, could you meet me in the antique shop. We could talk about what we are going to do about this attention-drawing mirror. I will make us a salad, and I will supply the wine.

"Vern, that would make a wonderful evening. I will bring the bread and cheese."

"Odalie, that sounds super. One more thing."

"OK, what's that, Vern."

"Odalie, I love you."

Odalie made no comment, but she was looking forward to the meeting with Vern and their mirror. Vernon was, too.

The evening of the meeting had a certain magic to it. Odalie was greeted at the antique shop's door by Vern. He hugged her and kissed her passionately on lips as soft as ruby-red rose petals. Both the greeter and his guest retired to a makeshift kitchen in the back of the shop. A small table set for two held a single candle, and that set the stage for what was to come. The candle's flickering seemed to rush both diners to years in the past when electricity had not yet been discovered, and the atmosphere established a perfect moment and blended in perfectly with their surroundings----implements from a past time. The wine further enhanced the setting and helped relax a couple drawing closer to one another. Light conversation took place. Friends were discussed, and when the meal had ended, the couple took chairs in front of the fabled mirror and its companion, the beer-hall sign from the 15th century. The solitary candle was the only lighting offered. Vernon said, "Odalie, do we need more light on the mirror?"

"Vern, that candle is just perfect. When you think of it, reflections made hundreds of years ago were lighted only by candles."

"That's true. I hadn't thought of that"

"Now, Sir, thinking back to what you said to me last night on the phone."

"Yes."

"You said that you loved me."

"Yes. I did, and I meant every word of it. I also said that the mirror was 'our' mirror. I meant that, too."

"Were you serious about both subjects?"

"Odalie, I have never been more serious about anything in my life. Forget the mirror. I am talking about you. You are more than I ever expected to find in France. You have enhanced my life. I want that to continue, and I want you to consider being with me for the rest of my life. When you get time, and do take your time, please give me your response to what I have suggested to you. I am asking you to…"

It that very moment, time seemed to freeze everyone in place except for the surface of the mirror. A shimmering took place on the surface of the glass, at first imperceptible, but bit by bit, the projection of a man in medieval clothing began to take shape against a solid black background. Neither Vernon nor Odalie moved nor spoke. Their eyes were transfixed on the figure which seemed to beckon to them, and then it abruptly disappeared. Odalie spoke first saying to a still-silent partner, "Vern, what just happened?"

It took a few seconds to catch his breath before he could speak. When he did, he said, "Odalie, are you OK?"

"Yes, Vern. Now tell me what we just experienced and saw with our own eyes."

"Odalie, I come from New Orleans. In that part of the States, Voodoo, the black arts and its variations are practiced and believed by a certain segment of the population. What we just witnessed, a character from another time and place, borders on the paranormal, something that cannot be significantly explained. If we tried to make sense of it, we might be slipping into paranoia."

"What are we going to do, Vern?"

"Odalie, we are going to sleep on it. I am going to walk you home right up to your door. Tomorrow, we, you and I, will be more able to make sense of what just happened, and we will do it together. Now, come with me. We both need rest."

42

Sometimes, when faced with the unexplainable and incomprehensible, it is up to you, the one faced with the mystery, to suggest an explanation. Vernon Sarvey, this young American expatriate living in a foreign country had never before witnessed anything as bizarre as the image he had seen in his antique mirror. Vernon believed in God and doing good instead of evil, and he believed that never straying from that belief had led him to Odalie Markette, this beautiful, voluptuous young woman who seemed to welcome his advances with open arms and other such appendages related to love making. But Vernon was sure of one thing---he was going to capitalize on his two-pronged good fortune; he was going to try to hold on to Odalie, and he was going to take advantage of the unknown.

Odalie had told Vernon about her successes with helping people achieve their dreams and aspirations. He knew about a certain male vocalist who, with Odalie's encouragement and help, had achieved prominence on the stage. Vernon was also aware of the young pianist who had blossomed under

Odalie's tutorage. Vern suspected that Odalie had shared some or the magic that was projected from his mirror, and now, he needed that strange expertise in his life. Vern Sarvey was going to ask Odalie to help him find and organize a small group of young thespians, school them, and direct them in giving small stage presentations of personages from French history in and around the city of Blois. Even Francois Villon, the great French poet and supposed author of the lost poem, *Le Pet au Diable,* 'The Devil's Fart', the device inscribed on the wooden beer-hall sign from the 15th century would come under scrutiny. Vernon couldn't wait to make two proposals to the woman he had come to love.

Two days later, and after some thought, Vernon arrived at Odalie's home, was welcomed immediately by the home's owner and said, "Odalie, I have two proposals I would like to make to you, and the first has to do with asking you for your help in establishing a small entertainment venue at the antique shop. Knowing you have the knack of pulling out excellence in those you have tutored, let me ask you this: could you work with me in getting a small acting group together to give a *son et lumiere* showing every two weeks at our antique center? We would use the format of what has been going on for years at the chateaux in the region. We would research characters from the history in the region, make a scrip, set it to music and entertain the public. Seeing the area's historic characters act out their parts, dressed in the clothing of the period would infuse an interest not only to tourists but to townspeople, too. We would use a mock-up of the mirror as a portal for the coming and going of the personalities. Of course, our original 15th century mirror would be one of the main attractions. What do you think?"

At first, Odalie was hesitant. It had been some time since she last squeezed excellence out of those she taught. But she did have confidence in her ability to conjure up enthusiasm and interest in her student proteges. Once her confidence had been mentally restored, Odalie responded, "Norm, I think you have a wonderful idea. I will help you in every way I can, of course. But you did say that you had two proposals to make to me. What was the second?"

Vern took his time. He and Odalie had retired to the little kitchen table in the back of her home. Odalie had taken a chair at her table. Vernon stood at the kitchen doorway and was looking at something at the foot of her chair. He said, "Odalie, did you break a jar or a glass lately in your kitchen? There is something at your feet. Let me get it for you." Vern made his way to Odalie's chair, bent down on one knee and said, "I've got it." In his hand, he held a beautifully cut diamond ring. Holding it up for her to see, he said, "Odalie Markette, will you, the most beautiful women my heart and eyes have ever known, become Mrs. Vernon Sarvey?"

In Odalie's response, there was no doubt that soon, the two star-crossed lovers would be man and wife.

43

Odalie had seen the often-staged Hollywood movie versions of marriage proposals and the television ads which pictured the man on his knee before a surprised smiling female. A smile came to her face, too, now that she was the subject of such an action. However, her smile turned to tears, and she looked down at Vernon and the ring in his hand and she said, "*Oui, trois fois oui, Vernon.*" The use of her native language expressed a total agreement that Odalie Markette would soon become Vernon Sarvey's wife.

Vernon's marriage proposal with all its intensions was consummated more than several times that evening. A recharged passion enhanced a strong desire to continue a relationship which, by all evidence, was stronger than ever. Both the proposer and the accepter of the future marriage slept late into the next day. When they did awaken, no time was wasted in setting into motion what had been discussed about making Vern's mirror into a social and entertainment venue.

The theater department at Grenoble University was contacted, and a request for those interested in summer employment as actors and actresses depicting historical figures from the past was posted. Flyers announcing the same information were placed in public places all over the city of Blois. By early May, ten or more probable actors had made it known that they were interested in the antique owner's project. Auditions were held, possible starting actors and actresses were hired, and practice began which would lead to a June 1st opening night.

Vernon had contacted some local carpenters and contracts for the construction of a small outdoor stage were signed. The acting platform would be very close to the antique shop entrance and would all easy positioning of the fabled mirror and other relics of interest. Odalie had researched the background of characters to be portrayed, and practice began. The title for the first-night's performance was, '*Le Portail du Miroir*'. The 'Mirror's Gateway' had already drawn the interest of almost everyone in Blois.

When June 1 arrived, ticket sales had already paid for the construction of the small stage and had compensated the actors who were going to bring Charles d'Orleans, Le Duc de Guise, Joan of Arc, Francois Villon and Catherine de Medicis back to life. The city streets of Blois were decorated, colorful signs and artwork were displayed, and everyone was ready to take part in the magic of seeing some of their French heroes speak for the first time in centuries.

44

On the eve of the first showing of this extravaganza on French history, June 1, the city streets of the town of Blois were alive with all sorts of animation. Colorful banners waved from open windows, street goers were talking excitedly about what they might see and hear at the up-coming event, and street venders were doing a lively business selling baguettes, cheeses and liquid refreshment. The organizers of the showing, Vernon and Odalie, were attending to last-minute adjustment to scenery and decorations of the stage. All was ready for present-day magic to reconstruct history.

At the program's opening, several hundred onlookers jammed the small square, carpenter-constructed stage just outside the entrance to the antique shop. Odalie had agreed to MC the evening's event, and the low-cut summer dress she wore guaranteed the interest of every male in the crowd. Her jewelry consisted of a thin gold neckless and a beautiful diamond engagement ring.

Odalie welcomed everyone to the evening performance, and she cited the names of several of the historic characters who would be brought to life and emerge through the mirror-like portal on stage. The original piece, the antique mirror itself, stood close by and could be clearly seen by everyone in the audience. And then, the program began. The first magically-revived personage was Charles d'Orleans, the prince/poet from the 15th century. Dressed in the costume of the period, the Duke gave the audience a sample of one of his poems, and then he introduced this protégé, Francois Villon, he, too, in period costume, and the greatest French poet made reference to the beer sign he was said to have stolen which now occupied the space alongside the fabled mirror. One by one, other historical characters made their way out of and back into the imaginatively-constructed faux looking glass.

After the first-night's showing, the proceeds from advanced sales, the evening performance and *pourboires* offered to performers, further shows throughout the summer were assured. The first night's work was a huge success. But at the very end of the show, when the last actor had gone back through the portal into the unknown, something took place on the surface of the genuine mirror; the entire surface of the glass began to shimmer, and what appeared to be a solitary figure waved a goodbye to the theater goers. Most people attributed that departing act as part of the electronics of the show and thought no more about the man in the mirror. That bit of abnormality was not lost on the promoters of the presentation; Odalie just nodded to Vernon and shrugged her shoulders in disbelief. The phenomenon they had just witnessed would be discussed later. Right now, a mopping up had to take place. Attendees at the performance had left behind a detritus of paper cups, napkins, plastic bottles and other personal discarded items. Once the stage area had been cleaned, Odalie and Vern had a class of wine and they toasted each other with a hearty *"Tchin, tchin"*. Vern spoke first with, "You saw it, too".

"Yes. Do you think it could have been ambient light coming from the candles we were using to show the mirror's surface?"

"Odalie, at this point, I haven't the slightest idea, and as I told you before, my belief in the supernatural is non-existent. But something did happen in our mirror. I cannot believe that tonight's presentation awakened the ghosts of those we portrayed on stage. In the future, both of us must observe and investigate such things if they happen again."

"I agree, Vern. Right now, we need rest. Tomorrow is another day."

Neither the host nor the hostess of the first performance of the *son et lumiere* rested that night. The concerns of strange sightings was washed away in a flood of passionate pleasure.

45

The weekly *son et lumiere* cultural and historical offerings continued throughout the month of July, and every so often toward the end of each production, one of the stage performers would make reference to what seemed to be a likeness of an historical character appearing on the surface of Vern's antique mirror. Vernon recorded these sightings brought to his attention, and he kept a journal in which period clothing, male or female personages and gestures were catalogued. Vernon would jokingly tell his theater cast presenters that he or she had done so well on stage that their work drew special recognition from the long-departed models they had portrayed. Vern always shared what he had heard from his cast to Odalie who, in spite of her religious upbringing, began to believe in the occult or suspect the playing of a ruse by one of the stage crew. In a discussion of what they had learned, Odalie and Vernon decided to contact a well-known French investigator of things labeled paranormal.

Between weekend theater productions, running an antique shop and socialization with friends and neighbors, Odalie and Vern spent some time in the local libraries informing themselves about mysterious and otherworldly occurrences. They looked into J.B. Rhine's book, 'Extrasensory Perception and Parapsychology' which introduced the researchers to psychic mediums. They investigated the author, Arthur Conan Doyle whose character, Sherlock Holmes dabbled in the paranormal. But it was the English-born Yvette Fielding and her TV show on ghost hunting which held their interest. Fielding believed in life after death. However, after all their research, Odalie and her fiancé, Vernon, were not yet quite convinced that their mirror and its history had been the source of anything from another world…until…

Until the week leading to the end of August which corresponded with the end of the summer programs of *son et lumiere* entertainment for tourists and inhabitants of the Loire Valley. During that time, Vernon suggested that he and Odalie discuss their marriage, where they would live, work and plan for the future. No fixed times had been established for the event, and it had not yet been decided where their vows would take place. Odalie was Catholic, and she had been a regular practitioner of her religion at the cathedral in Blois. She did not make any religious demands on Vern. He believed in God, and he would honor any choice his future wife might make. But the last performance of the summer was about to take place, and time for personal decisions was in short supply.

46

Summer was coming to an end, tourists were returning to their home countries and students were again getting ready for fall classes at university and public schools. Cast members who played roles in the *son et lumieres* were returning to classes. But theater presentations had been so popular that Vernon and Odalie were already equipped with enough funds for next summer's productions, and their theater staff would have little trouble paying for their fall semester at school.

The last show of the summer was to take place on August 27 on a Saturday, and everything was in place. The wooden-constructed portal was polished and its twin, the original 15th century mirror was on display nearby. The show started, and judging by the applause after each spot in the theater guide, the audience approved enthusiastically. But this last show of the summer would leave the audience and one of its sponsors in awe.

Just as the last performer was doing his rendering of Francois Villon, the actor finished his soliloquy on the poet's lost poem, 'Le Pet-au-Diable', 'The Devil's Fart'. The crowd roared in laughter at what was supposedly the famous poet's words. The actor performing the role took his bows and stepped through the well-constructed portal to the past. But what happened next was unexpected; Odalie stepped up on the state, blew her fiancé a kiss and disappeared into the unknown along with the last stage presenter. The show was over.

When Vern, the co-sponsor of the summer's entertainment on his outdoor stage, saw his fiancée disappear with all the other stage crew through the faux portal, he thought to himself, *'What a stroke of theatrical genius! I would never have thought of that.'* Vernon could not wait until he could congratulate his dark-haired beauty for her *coup de theatre*. He immediately went to the rally area behind the stage's portal. All the summer's stage practitioners of his amateur theater would gather there for a last hoorah before going on their way to their prospective homes and schools. At the rendezvous area, Odalie was nowhere to be seen.

Vernon's first move, once he could not locate his fiancée, was to locate the last actor, the young man who had interpreted the character, Francois Villon. He had been the last to pass through the portal before Odalie. Villon's imitator was easy to find; he was surrounded by admiring cast members. Vernon stepped up to him and said, "Did Odalie follow you through the portal at the end of the play? Have you seen her?" Villon's interpreter replied, "I saw no one behind me. I was alone after passing through the portal." At that very moment, a coldness seemed to sweep up across the back of Vern's neck, and he shuttered as if gripped by an icy hand. It was at that moment that panic began to play its role in the missing co-sponsor of the summer's spectacular.

Vernon ran back to his little office at the rear of the antique store. No one was there. He then searched his small bedroom, its closets and his small one-shower bath. Again, he was alone in his home. He had seen Odalie's friend, Monique, the tea-room owner in the evening's crowd. Thinking that she might stll be around, he went looking for her. A minute or two later, Vern found Monique in a cluster of the evening's attendees, and they were discussing the program's presentations. Vern walked up to the group and said to Monique, "Excuse me, Monique. Have you seen Odalie? I can't seem to find her." Monique responded, "No, Vern. I lost sight of her the moment she disappeared going into the portal. That was a nice touch for the co-sponsor to pull off right at the end of the show." Under his breath, Vern said to himself, '*I thought so, too, but that was unrehearsed.*' For the very first time in his life, Vern Sarvey, American expatriate, found himself without answers and very much alone.

In spite of the fact that cell phones were carried by everyone including school-age children, Vern had forgotten to use his. He pulled it out, pressed in Odalie's number and heard, 'The party's cell-phone storage is full. No message will be recorded.' Small cliques of theater goes waited to compliment Vern on his big success at the theater. He avoided these groups and made his way on foot to Odalie's little home just blocks away. It took almost no time to reach Odalie's front door. Vern had his own key, turned the lock and entered the foyer of Odalie's home calling out, "Odalie, are you here?" Vern inspected each room of the home. He found no one. The little house was completely empty.

For the next hour, Vern walked the streets of Blois looking for his fiancée. He walked the path which ran along the river, checked the little squares and parks, but he encountered nothing but citizens out enjoying the evening. Odalie Markette, the last person to pass through the faux portal to the unknown, was gone.

47

The moment when Vernon saw his co-sponsor of the summer's pageant disappear along with the last stage presenter through the faux portal, he thought to himself, *What a stroke of genius. I would never have thought of doing that.* He could not wait until he could congratulate Odalie, his dark-haired beauty, on her *coup de theatre.* He hurried back stage to the little area where the summer's theater players were gathered in celebration of their successful season. Odalie was not among the boisterous group.

Vern's first move, once he could not locate his partner, went directly up to the young man who had preceded Odalie through the portal. When that cast member acknowledged the antique shop owner, he asked, "What did you think of our finale?" Vern said, "That's why I am here. Have you seen Odalie? She followed you through the portal." The actor replied, "No, I was the last to leave the stage. Is she missing?" It was at that moment that Vern felt a sudden coldness run up the back of his neck. He did not panic. After all, a lot of people had been in and around the stage area at the end of the show, and he had not searched his office.

In less than a minute, Vern entered his antique shop, went directly to his office and found it empty. He checked the other rooms, his bedroom, the little bath and the small kitchen where he and Odalie had prepared meals. No one occupied the shop but the owner. His next move was to send a call to Odalie through his cell phone. It rang, and a voice answered saying, "The phone-message bank if full. No messages can be taken." In a flash, Vern was out the door of his shop and on his way to Odalie's home just two blocks away. With his own key, he opened Odalie's front door, searched every room and found no one.

During the next hour and what must have seemed to be an eternity, Vern patrolled the streets of Blois like a Marine in the sandbox of Afghanistan looking for some sign of life with Odalie. He walked the waterfront and took paths which led by the river. Apart from midnight lovers, Vern's best friend, lover and co-sponsor of the summer's theater productions was either invisible or not at all in the area.

Vernon waited for what he thought would be the appropriate amount of time before he made a missing person's claim at the local gendarmerie. In the United States, he had learned that the local police would not move into action until a twenty-four-hour period had passed, and even then, excuses would be voiced such as, "She is probably shopping or visiting a friend." But Vern was not in the United States and he was scolded by French police for waiting so long before reporting that his fiancée was missing.

He was told, "You know, Monsieur, women in France have their secret lives, too." When Vern told the gendarmes that she was last seen stepping through a faux portal to the past, raised eyebrows signaled that the missing person's report was perhaps the fantasy of the seeker. Vern was dismissed with a curt, "Every woman returns sooner or later."

On a whim, Vernon made a decision to stop in and talk to Odalie's friend, Monique. Her tea room was doing well. Customers filled most of the small tables, and the tea room owner was supervising her workers as Vern walked in the store. Vern took a table, and when she got a break, Monique joined him and they shared a cup of tea. Monique spoke first, and she said, "Vern, were you and Odalie having a problem recently?" Vern's eyes opened wide and he replied, "If anything, we were closer than ever. You do know, she accepted my proposal for marriage, and we worked together well on this summer's theater production."

"Did you set a date for the marriage?"

"No, we were so busy with the shows, and there did not seem to be a minute for us to consider a thing other than making sure we had a successful first-running of the history review on stage."

"Vernon, a little advice. Make time for Odalie."

"Gladly. But I must first find her."

"Vern, are you certain you want to find her?"

"Monique, If I do not find her, I will sell my business and return stateside."

"OK, I can help you, but you must ask no questions. Go to your shop, and on Wednesday evening, after store hours, seat yourself next to the ancient mirror and wait for as long as it takes. While you are there, talk to the mirror as though it, too, was human, and tell it why you are there."

"Monique, tell me what's going on here. What do you know that I don't?"

"Vern, I must get back to work. Please do what I say."

With that, Monique returned to her employees and worked right alongside them. Vern returned to his antique shop.

In the days leading up to Monique's suggested meeting, like others who at one time or another found themselves abandoned or suffering the loss of a loved one for not apparent reason, Vernon began to blame himself, and he questioned what he might have done to cause Odalie to avoid him. He questioned whether or not he had given Odalie enough leadership roles in the development of the summer's spectaculars on stage. Could he have been too passionate in his love making to this young French woman? That could not possibly be the case; Odalie had shown herself to be a most-willing and adept person when in bed or out. Vern was at a loss as to what might have caused her absence.

Vern busied himself in his work at the antique shop in the days leading up to the Wednesday meeting. He inventoried his collections, looked into estate sales and tidied up shelves and displays. This summer's stage platform was dismantled and stored for the future. He then placed a call to his father in New Orleans. Vern did not relate the recent missing-person details with his friend, Odalie. Vern related to his father that he had recently become engaged and that all was well in his love life. He even believed that most of what he said was true.

48

Wednesday came like a rocket. Vernon worked throughout the day in spite of his being preoccupied mentally. There was one subject on his mind, and it had to do with relocating the woman with whom he had lived the better part of a year. He prepared himself. He scrubbed, combed, dressed in casual but good-looking slacks and sport shirt. White shirts and ties were for store business. This evening's business, he hoped, would be total pleasure. Vern was up for just about anything with the exception of learning that Odalie had been disfigured in some freak accident. He did tell himself that, no matter what, he was ready to see his fiancée as soon as possible.

Around 8 P.M., Vern readied himself in front of the antique mirror, and he contemplated the thing as if it were some angry being ready for a duel. He half expected some specter to appear emerging from the glass reaching for him and wanting to drag him back into the glass. But Vernon had played football at Tulane University in New Orleans, and he could give as good as he got. Just as he was ready to do battle with whatever he encountered, Odalie, dressed in a beautiful evening gown displaying her formidable well-turned figure, stepped from behind the ancient mirror and said, "Hello, Vern."

Vern's first thoughts, those of a distraught lover, had him ready to run to the feet of the woman he loved, take her into his arms and declare undying love. But Odalie held up her hand and stopped on movement he might have had in mind and said, "Wait! There are things I must tell you first. Please sit down and listen to me." Vern obeyed immediately.

Odalie began by saying that she still was unsure about what had happened to her the last night of the summer theater. She told Vern that she could not explain what had happened to her or what had taken place in the days following her disappearance. Although she did not know how it might have taken place, she said that she felt as though she had experienced an out-of-the-body sensation, that she had never before felt so unable to control her thoughts or her steps. Odalie added that as much as she enjoyed the fruit of the grape and sharing it with Vern, she hadn't touched a drop the entire day of the last show. Then, she said, "Now, Vern, you must believe me. I do not believe in the supernatural; science does not allow me to slip into trying to explain the unexplainable. However, the moment I stepped back through our faux portal, something, a spirit, a whisp of excitement of the moment, or something…took hold of me, led me off and away from the stage, and I ended up in one of the alcoves of the chateau of Blois. And, I was not alone."

Vern just listened. He shook his head in disbelief, and Odalie continued her story saying, "Vern, are you familiar with the story of the Arabian Nights?"

"You mean the one where Shahrazad told tales in order to marry the one she choose and not her father's choice?"

"Yes. At the chateau, I was not alone. The person who led me there, kept me there, fed me and talked to me was, of this I am almost sure, the 15th century poet, Francois Villon."

"Odalie, what gave you that impression?"

"The man, dressed in the clothing typical of the time period said that he wanted us to do something with his sign, the one we bought from a small antique shop."

"The Devil's Fart?"

"Yes, that's the one. And, this is what he wants us to do."

49

Just as Odalie was about to continue her extraordinary explanation of her disappearance, Vernon moved from his spot in his store to the side of the woman he loved, took her into his arms and hugged her as though she represented a long-lost member of his family. He kissed her and said,

"Odalie, let's talk about this in our kitchen over a cup of tea. You can tell me more when you are feeling more at home and at peace with me next to you." Odalie's tears signaled that Vernon's suggestion was exactly what she needed at the moment, and they both settled down around a small kitchen table to talk.

"Odalie, how did Monique come into the story?"

"She had been looking for me, too, and something, some magical thing brought her to the chateau in the middle of the night. She is such a good friend, Vern."

In a calmer setting, and thanks to Vern's sensitive recognition of stress, Odalie was able to make more sense of what had happened to her. In her talk with Monique earlier, she had informed her friend from the tea room that she thought she had encountered the French poet, Francois Villon. She told Vern, "He even had recited his *'Ballade des dames du temps jadis'* reciting the famous line, *'Mais ou sont les neiges d'autan',* (But where are the snows of yesteryear?). He used medieval French and Latin, and he issued a wish."

"He requested something from you. Odalie?"

"Well, Vern, as bizarre as it might seem, I think this shadowy character was talking about his tavern sign, the one he was acclaimed to have stolen with his band of rogues."

"What did he say, Odalie?"

"I think he was saying that we should make use of the sign in your business, something to the effect of using that piece of history to enhance your and perhaps my life. Vern, tell me that I am not going completely mad. The poet or whatever he was had intended to say more, but Monique appeared in the part of the chateau where I was located, and the poet's image dissipated as if in a puff of smoke."

"Odalie, as strange as your story might sound, none of us know what the world around us might conjure up. You must know by this time, with what we have done together, seen and felt, that if you told me you could fly, I would say, 'How high can you go?' You are the best thing that has ever happened to me, and knowing you is like living life on a movie set. And, I want more."

"Thank you, Vern. What are you going to do with me?"

"Well, my love, that will come later. But right now, I am going to let you get some rest. Then, I am going to take you to dinner where we can talk and decide whether we can figure out what we might have been asked to do."

Odalie was escorted to her home, put to bed, and before he left, Vern leaned down and kissed Odalie say, "Sleep well. I will return early tomorrow."

Sleepless nights were not usually part of Vern Sarvey's life. As a youth and again into adolescent and young adult growth, he had worked hard and done well so that doubt, unaccomplished goals and minor setbacks did not wrack his brain at night. But now, after listening to and contemplating the trials and tribulations of his lover, Odalie, sleep deprivation invaded him like some swarm of hornets. His questions had no conceivable answers, so he focused on what might come next----determining what it was which had to take place next.

Vern wondered what entity, thing, or specter had entered his and Odalie's life. What was the message given concerning the tavern sign and its purpose, and if it had a purpose, how was it going to be put into action. Vern did know that all this and more would be discussed with Odalie. Even Monique, Odalie's friend and tea-room owner, might be part of the group looking into the next steps they would take. Hours passed, and sleep did not come.

50

The next morning, in spite of his sleepless night, Vern dragged himself out of bed and went directly to Odalie's little cottage. He carried with him fresh croissants and hot coffee, let himself in and found Odalie already out of bed and sitting at her kitchen table. She wore a big, appreciative smile to welcome her lover into her home. Vern, recognizing his warm greeting said, "Ah, fresh croissants and coffee does bring out your beautiful smile." Odalie had an immediate comeback saying, "Vernon Sarvey, it is the sight of you that brings smiles to my face. You have a way of doing that often, too, don't you." Vern's reply was, "Why, Mademoiselle, whatever do you imply?"

After affectionate hugs, the consumption of coffee and croissants, It was decided that an evening dinner celebration at an upscale restaurant would be appropriate. Monique would be included in the dinner party, and the three of them could perhaps put together the puzzle given them by the mystery person from the mirror. Dinner reservations were made, Monique confirmed her invitation, and all three of the newly-minted musketeers looked forward to their evening get together.

The triumvirate of Odalie, Vernon and Monique made their way from Odalie's little cottage to the upscale restaurant, *La Grenouillere,* 'The Frog Pond' at precisely 8 P.M. The group was immediately seated at an outdoor table which opened onto a little pond, and to no one's surprise, several large amphibians were sitting calmly on the rocks lining the sides of the pond. Vern commented, "Would you look at that. Living specimens advertising the restaurant's name." Odalie's come-back was, "If I order *cuisses de grenouille,* I hope it's not one of those little guys." Monique giggled and added, "They are so cute, but I would eat them anyway." Vern had the last word with, "Bon appetite, Monique."

The sommelier explained the wine chart, and then passed the torch to the head waiter. After a perusal of the menu, meals were ordered. Not one of the three diners ordered frogs legs for dinner. The proximity of the real McCoy was too close for mental comfort. Everyone agreed that the choice of the restaurant was perfect. Once the hors-d'oeuvres and main course had been consumed and enjoyed, the wine steward returned, wine was ordered, and the conversation having to do with the mystery man of the mirror began.

For more than several hours, the three late-night diners discussed the present, future and the past. Restaurant owners and their personnel did not disturb the tete-a-tete going on. They busied themselves with tasks concerning closing the restaurant. After it was all said and done, some decisions were made and agreed upon. There would not be any deceit, and the public would not be duped into believing in voodoo or the supernatural. The citizenry of the city of Blois would not be told that some unbelievable and misunderstood entity had invaded their premises, and that the antique shop was not victimized by ghosts.

Those who inhabited the area and who dabbled in the unknown were invited to visit and study both the 15th century mirror and what was presumed to be a tavern sign stolen by the French poet, Villon. Purveyors of the bizarre were invited to scrutinize Vernon's entire collection of items from the past by simply registering, free of charge, and peruse up close the most talked-about pieces. And there were consequences of that invitation.

In the coming months, true believers in the occult, the supernatural and the unexplainable joined amateur historians who flocked to the antique store as if they were wild geese coming in to roost. Sales of long overlooked antiques mounted, and profits rose from each sale. Revenues from such interest assured a profitable enterprise for years to come. Books were written and published about the strange goings on at a little antique shop in the city of Blois. Most of the stories written bordered on fantasy, but for a true believer, nothing was beyond the pale.

During all that time, Odalie grew closer, if such a thing was possible, to her lover/owner of the antique store. Vernon's love making was more passionate than ever, and the late-night sounds of that passion filled the air in and around both the homes of the sound makers. None of their neighbors complained. After all, it was taking place in France.

51

In the weeks and months after having decided to encourage public opinion about relics shown at Vern's antique shop, supposed sightings and hallucination-prone discoveries popped up everywhere. Pub conversations, open-air market shoppers and library goers were talking about what could be magic in the city. Hundreds of scribbled messages about strange happening in and around the city's antique shop began to appear on billboards, common areas and street corners. In almost every European language, people swore that they had encountered the ghost in the mirror, and some even detailed conversations they had shared with something or someone. A few young women hinted that they had received a proposal…turned down, of course, to meet at some late-night rendezvous.

The more-prominent postings of such fantastic occurrences took place in the local newspapers, and before long, *Le Monde*, one reputable French newspaper, ran a full-page coverage of the goings-on in the city of Blois. Vernon called Odalie's attention to the monetary offers for purchase of both the fabled mirror and pub sign, and the prices given were in the millions of euros. If they had wanted to, accepting such purchase offers would make the American antique dealer and his close French friend millionaires. But the two entrepreneurs had other plans---they were going to get married. But the story of Odalie Markette does not end here, and the two lovers were not going to ride off into the sunset like some 1950' American film stars. They had things to do in their city.

52

Old habits die hard. They have a life of their own. Things done well and enjoyed are apt to be remembered and repeated. Odalie Markette was a creature of her own making. She had that special gift, what it took to motivate people and bring out the best in them. Whether it was the mastery of what some musicians do or whether it was the proprietor of a small tea room in some city, Odalie inspired. She was able to enhance one's ability to excel in a field of their choosing. Sometimes profitable, sometimes not, Odalie Markette thrived on her ability to improve the lives of other people. Now, at this time in her life, not fully understanding it, she had another pupil, a man with whom she had fallen in love---Vernon Sarvey, the American antique dealer.

Sarvey, this American from New York and New Orleans, had already achieved a good deal of success in his field; he knew the value of old things, and antiques offered a good source of income. But little did Vern know that he would soon acquire a special skill, one which most men only dreamed about---the allosexual experience of being the perfect lover. Oh, sure, Vernon was capable in the bedroom. With Odalie, love making was easy; her beauty inspired, enticed and excited a physical passion comparable to a k-9 in heat.

Odalie took her new pupil under her wing and began his schooling. Subtle hints and suggestions from the teacher began to show promise in the student. Vernon Sarvey was learning the art of making a woman lose all her fears about sexual union. Odalie taught Vernon how a soft touch in the right places could stimulate and coax. Vernon learned that a scent of a woman could telegraph acceptance and invite a spur of the moment relaxation of tension.

Vernon was the consummate pupil. But it was Odalie who controlled the on/off switch on love making. A look, a sultry smile, a loosely-fitting piece of clothing might be all it took to unloose the hunger of human desire. And, as one might expect, such teaching, perfect practice and trial runs could result in pregnancy. Odalie, the consummate researcher/teacher, outlined, explained and demonstrated the oral sex terms, fallatio and cunnilingus to an amazed but willing-to-learn Vernon Sarvey. And, it did enhance ability to stimulate, much to the joy of both teacher and student. At such times, both participants in this act of learning were in need of rest. Two children were the outcome of experimentation. One, a girl, was named, Mauvaise. The other, a boy, Vernon Jr., one year younger than his sister, became playmates in their father's antique shop. The mother and father, both involved in the operation of their business, would often hear a third voice in their shop, a voice of a man. When quizzed by the parents as to who the third voice was, both Mauvaise and Vernon Jr. gave the same answer, "He dresses funny and plays games with us. He comes right out of the mirror, and he always says that he wants his pub sign back"

53

"Out of the mouths of babes..." is an idiom familiar to Vernon Sarvey. His maternal grandmother had used that term when a precocious young Vernon would interject his thoughts into an adult conversation. Vern had become aware of Psalms 8:2 after his grandmother pointed out its meaning, and he had never forgotten it. Was he disturbed that his children, now aged 4 and 5, had perhaps experienced a flash from the past, a step out of the unknown and into the present? Not at first. After all, children overhear things in their meandering around the home. The supposed appearance of a specter coming from an antique mirror was, at times, had been the topic of conversation at in-the-home and other social gatherings. Kids repeat things as they learn one language or another. Vern and Odalie's children spoke both French and English, and Vern needed more information about this latest verbal sidebar.

Vernon did not at first alert his beloved wife that their children had supposedly become aware of things which took place in the past. Children love the mystique of rumors, and an antique-seller's home is full of such things. A few days later, Vern did share with his wife, Odalie, what the children had reported. Odalie shared her husband's opinion that children, needing to prove their place in the home, sometimes repeat and exaggerate the slightest item once heard in an adult conversation. But Vernon, now the consummate father, decided to do some investigation on his own.

Vernon's plan was laid out like a military campaign. He sat up a listening post close to the proverbial mirror. A comfortable chair/recliner was provided by his wife, Odalie, for she, too, was part of Vern's forward-observer team. Odalie wanted to believe in this stake out maneuver, but Vern knew that she needed sleep in the late hours of the night; their children would require attention. All the stake outs were to take place in the late evening and early-morning hours; ghosts, if they did exist, were seldom if ever recorded during daylight hours.

For the first few nights watch, nothing happened. No flickering of the lights, no disturbances took place on the mirror's glass, and no strange sounds were recorded. On the fourth night, however, something did happen. Just as Vern was nodding off to sleep in his chair, he heard a voice.

"Monsieur is waiting for me?"

Vern rubbed the sleep from his eyes and looked at the surface of the mirror. On its surface was a man dressed in what looked to be medieval clothing including a funny-looking shepherd's cap. The man wore a smile, and he seemed to be enjoying his unsuspected arrival. Van spoke saying, "Sir, I don't know who you are or from where you come, but let me bid you welcome. Who are you?"

"Oh, you know who I am. That I speak English should not surprise you. Over the last five hundred years, I have had the time to learn hundreds of the world's languages. I have come for my tavern sign."

"I understand. But why would you want it now, and how are you going to get it to where you are now?"

"My boys took the trouble to rip off the sign from a very rowdy pub frequented by wenches of all kinds of shapes and sizes. It's the memory of such places that makes me want to keep the sign. We need to know where it is and that it will be kept safe."

"May I keep it for you?"

"Yes, but you must never sell it. That would not be good for you or family."

"I understand. It has come to my attention, Sir, that you met my children."

"Yes. They are wonderful children. They believe in things. I read poetry to them."

"Did you read to them your long-lost last poem?"

"Oh, no, that poem is not for children's ears. Do you know the poem, Sir?"

"No one does. It was said to be your last."

"Partly true. A couple of them rotted away while I was in *les oubliettes.*"

"What are *les oubliettes?*"

"A hole in the ground where they throw innocent prisoners and forget them. Would you like to hear what people say was my last poem?"

"*Le pet au Diable,* The Devil's Fart? Why yes, and I would like my wife, Odalie, to hear it, too."

"Yes, Madame Sarvey and I are already acquainted. She is the beautiful women I abducted from the stage performance this past summer."

"When could you read for us, Sir?"

"Tomorrow night would be good. I must tell my boys that our sign is safe first."

"That would be great. What will we call you, Sir?"

Call me 'Vagabond'. The name begins with the same letter as does my last name, and it fits my new life style."

"Tomorrow night, then. *Au revoir, Monsieur.*"

In an instant, 'V' had disappeared from the mirror's surface. Odalie learned immediately of the late-night sighting. She listened as Vern outlined his meeting, and she expressed neither surprise nor shock. After all, she had already met this stranger from the past, and she had an idea of just who he was. Then, she turned toward her husband and said, "Vern, can we trust this person?"

"I don't see why not. And, he seems to be locked in place in the mirror…for now. We have nothing to fear. He's going to read his last unpublished poem to us."

"Do you mean…?

"You guessed it---The Devil's Fart."

54

That night and the following day melted like butter on a hot day's picnic table. Before they knew it, Mauvaise and her brother, Vern, Jr., were fed and put to bed. Vernon Sr. and Odalie made themselves ready for their midnight or early-morning visitor. Very little was said between husband and wife during their late-night vigil. Both were afraid to speak out of fear of losing their minds. The magic of it all---the request for another tete-a-tete with a supernatural visitor---brought the husband and wife solidly together.

At approximately the same time that the previous meeting took place between this mystery person and Vernon, the surface of the mirror became turbulent, and 'V', last-night's mystery man, became clear. The person in the mirror, still wearing 15th century clothing, bowed to Odalie and said, "Madame, we meet again, and you are as beautiful as ever." Odalie nodded her appreciation of the verbal comment and answered, "Thank you for not scaring our children. They are amazed with a man who speaks from a mirror." The mystery man answered with "Meeting and playing with your children was an unexpected pleasure, Madame."

Odalie again took over the conversation and said, "I have been told that you will recite a poem for us this evening."

"You are correct, Madame. But first, allow me to explain why the poem was written and what is implied in its wording." Vernon added his thoughts by saying, "That, Monsieur 'V', would please us." 'V' continued with, "First of all, when things do not go off as planned or something interferes with the smoothness of an issue, something which cannot always be explained, a sinister other person is sometimes the cause of the mishap; the Devil is usually the cause of that breakdown. At times, some of us, my gang members included, believe that the Devil himself is at fault. The first sign of trouble is the stench of the air which surrounds you. It reeks of an unknown source. Quite frankly, it is the Devil releasing air from his arse; it's the Devil's Fart. That's the title of my last poem. I shall recite it here in your language; 15th century French might be a little too demanding to understand."

With that, the visitor from the mirror took out a piece of parchment and began to read:

The Devil's Fart

When the cold wind blows and you are covered with snow,
And all about you smells rotten, nasty and tart,
Then you, good Prince, know and feel that you should depart,
Take up cloak, hat, shoes and leave that place not too slow,
For what your nose detects, Sir, It's the Devil's Fart.

Go here, go there, choose a lonely, safe pub or bar,
Don't tarry, do it quickly and don't go far,
Make haste, do it wisely, don't tip the apple cart,
It's not the mind that steers false, It's the nose by far,
For what your nose detects, Sir, It's the Devil's Fart.

When in doubt, no clue given, and yes, you've been smitten,
That bouquet you sense dear Prince, It's no small kitten,
Step back, don't dare breathe, take a moment and listen,
Don't question, turn around quick, It's not a friend at heart,
For what your nose detects, Sir, It's the Devil's Fart.

It's here, it's there, and so, it lingers everywhere,
No wind, no breeze can influence its full depart,
For what your nose detects, Sir, It's the Devil's fart.

At the end of the man in the mirror's recitation, both Vernon and Odalie applauded cautiously and smiled their approval. Odalie asked the poet, "Sir, what you just offered is well done and much appreciated, but tell us please that you will not divulge any such thing to our children; they do not yet have your worldly experience and flair in speech." The poet responded, "Madame Sarvey, inflicting harm on a child's upbringing and knowledge is not my intention. However, at a later age, when they might need such an exposure, I will be at their service. Let me add that I find it sad that I could not have used my 15th century French and Latin in the poem. It, too, uses the alexandrine twelve-syllable line." With that last statement from the man in the mirror, his image faded back into time, and Odalie and Vern were left alone. Both the mother and father went to bed and immediately fell into the confines of comfortable sleep.

Epilogue

The hours, days, months and years which followed the poetry recitation saw amazing and wonderful things. Almost at will, Vernon, the American, and Odalie, the French beauty and true believer of things not normal, could coax out of the past an entity willing to be called forth. Many night conversations revealed much about 'V' and his life. He told his listeners about his meeting French royalty, his dealings with street-wise thugs and how he lost his life over the criticism of one of his poems, 'The Devil's Fart', in a back-street tavern. Light was thrown upon the 15th-century court life and the backroom bordellos of the period. But it was the Sarvey family future which benefitted most from this unusual association with a figure from the past.

Both Mauvaise and Vernon Jr. completed their Bacs and went on to graduate school where they excelled in medieval studies and French history. Their professors were amazed with their insight into 15th-century history and beyond. They, too, had been schooled by the man they called, 'V'. Although he never said it, everyone in the Sarvey family knew that they had been having conversations with the most-famous French poet, Francois Villon.

Nothing was ever shared with others concerning the late-night meetings with this stranger from the past. Although she was Odalie's best friend, Monique, the tea-room owner, was never told of 'V's comings and goings; one's sanity is more assured if secrets are kept close to the vest. Vernon's antique business prospered so well that many in his profession thought that he might have had agents in every department in France. Vernon never revealed that he did have a special friend who knew where old things were buried. In late-night dinners years after the children had left the family nest, Odalie and Vernon would question their own sanity. After all, it is not a wise thing to admit that you have been having conversations with a poet who was over five-hundred years old.

FIN